KU-745-952

GREEN SKIES AT NIGHT

When a wide-ranging Green Skies weather phenomenon threatens the people of Tulsa, Oklahoma with destruction, it's up to meteorologist Amber Devane to warn them. The trouble is, the local media don't believe her predictions. She must put aside her recovery from an operation to save her family and her county. Aided by school-friend Ryan, a native American astronomer, the two of them must fight the tumultuous weather and prejudices as well as struggle with their own whirlwind budding romance ...

ALAN C. WILLIAMS

GREEN SKIES AT NIGHT

Complete and Unabridged

LINFORD
Leicester

First published in Great Britain in 2020

First Linford Edition
published 2021

Copyright © 2020 by DC Thomson & Co. Ltd.,
and A C Williams
All rights reserved

*A catalogue record for this book is available
from the British Library.*

ISBN 978–1–4448–4723–9

Published by
Ulverscroft Limited
Anstey, Leicestershire

Printed and bound in Great Britain by
TJ Books Ltd., Padstow, Cornwall

This book is printed on acid-free paper

KENT
ARTS & LIBRARIES

1

Blue Skies and Fluffy Clouds

I awoke to the sound of Emma jumping onto my bed. The exuberance of youth.

'Mommy, Mommy. Grandpa and Granny are taking me on a picnic at the park. Are you coming, too?'

I rubbed the sleep from my eyes, struggling to sit up and give my daughter a kiss. A hug was out of the question, at least until the stitches healed. But how do you explain that to a four-year-old girl, full of love and energy?

My own Mom knocked on the door before putting her head around. 'There you are, you naughty girl. You realise that Mommy isn't well. Please come here, chicken.'

She smiled apologetically at me, brushing her dark, wavy hair to one side of her tanned face. She was always working outside on these warm, spring days, usually without a hat or sun-screen. 'Sorry about that, Amber. One minute she was there and the next …'

'It's OK, Mom. I know she can be a handful. It's time for me to rise and shine, anyway.'

Rising was one thing. Shining? I'd have to see.

I sat up to swing my legs from under the sheets. Emma stood back, remembering the explanation that Mommy wasn't the fun-loving Mommy she'd been two months before. My gaunt appearance had brought some tears when I'd first returned from hospital.

I'd tried to explain that I was still Mommy but I'd been ill. When Joshua had walked away from us, I'd had to return to my parents' farm near to Tulsa, with my beautiful daughter in tow. Most of the locals called it T-Town as it was named Tulsey Town way back when.

Mom stepped into the room to assist me to my feet. Bless her heart, so did Emma, doing her best to be as helpful.

'Hell,' I said, far too loudly for little

ears. The pain was excruciating. I almost collapsed back onto the bed, my legs feeling like jelly.

Mom gave me a disapproving stare.

'Language please, Amber.'

'Sorry, Mom. She's heard worse, mainly from Joshua but I'm no angel, either. In any case, Emma understands. She won't be swearing in class when she starts elementary school … wherever that might be.'

I crossed my fingers, hopeful that Emma did understand that swearing was wrong. Whoever said that bringing up children was easy, obviously had never had any.

I hobbled over to my slippers while Mom helped me with my bathrobe. At least my nightie was respectable in her eyes. To me it was dowdy and I'd be better off in a potato sack, but my favourite, silky ones were packed away. No point dressing up for a man who'd dumped me when I'd needed him most.

My mom had always regarded him as trailer trash. A shame that it had taken me so long to realise she was right.

After a visit to the bathroom and a scrub up, I breathed deeply, put on my cheeriest face and went into the kitchen. Mom, Dad and Emma were already tucking in.

'Howdy, sweetheart,' said Dad, hopping up to help with my chair. Everyone was dressed apart from me. Emma had milk and Rice Bubbles on her chin and I smiled as Mom reached over to wipe them off with a napkin.

'Feeling better today?' he continued. 'You're getting some colour back in those cheeks.'

'Okie-dokie,' I replied, relaxing back into old habits. To say that in Texas would instantly brand me an Oklahoman and would often lead to some half-wit cowboy bursting into a verse of that damn musical that had become the bane of my life.

As for me looking better? He wasn't lying exactly; more like a disingenuous statement or what Mom called a 'lily-white lie'. I'd just come from the mirror over the sink and been confronted with my ghostly, sullen-eyed, skeletal reflection.

Plus, my long, blondish hair needed a decent shampoo. Maybe I'd try that today, by myself after everyone had gone and Mom wasn't around to fuss over me. It was time I started returning to the woman I'd been before the diagnosis.

I sat down, grateful for the padded chair. Heavens above. Ten minutes and a walk of twenty yards had left me exhausted. Would I ever recover my strength?

'Would you like me to cook some bacon and eggs, Amber? Or perhaps flapjacks?' Mom offered. She was right, I needed to eat properly, although the thought of the smell of grease made me stifle a retch.

'No thanks. Just some cereal like you guys are having. Maybe some toast.'

Sitting opposite Emma, I was pleased to see her appetite wasn't diminished. The move from big-city Galveston in Texas to a very rural farm outside Tulsa would have been traumatic; being ripped from the only home she'd known and her daddy at the same time. At least she was familiar with this ranch, having visited it many times in her short life. It would be her permanent home now, at least for the foreseeable future.

My daughter reached out to take her glass of orange in both hands as I'd taught her. She took a mouthful then wiped her mouth with the back of her hand, as I had definitely not taught her. Dad, seeing Mom's disapproving stare, did the same. Emma gave a cheeky smile.

'Use your cloth napkin, please, young lady,' Mom suggested gently. 'As for you, Barry Devane, you should know better too. Honestly, it was hard enough with one child in this house before. With two of you, I'm going to have my work cut out.'

Emma followed her instruction before apologising. 'Sorry, Granny. I forgotted.' Then she stood and carried her dirty dishes to the sink, one by one.

'Are you ready, Grandpa?'

Dad took his dishes, too.

'Ready for what, my love?' I asked Emma. She was keen to get going.

'We is fixing to fetch the eggs from the hen house, Mommy. And see the new chickens what have hatched.' Her little eyes lit up and she clapped her hands in anticipation.

'Just don't get dirty. Either of you,' Mom admonished them.

'Yes, Granny,' said Emma.

'Yes, Granny,' mimicked Dad. My daughter giggled at the loving banter.

She was dressed in her floral best, ready for the picnic adventure. I could kiss Dad for taking her under his wing now that Joshua had made it clear that he didn't want anything to do with us. I still couldn't believe my ex's insensitivity. It was one thing to dismiss me from his life once I'd told him I had this debilitating illness; but to have chosen to give up any right to see his daughter was the most upsetting part of our break-up.

Our life together had been a mockery, his protestations of undying love a fabrication for his own ends. He and Emma had never been close. Even so, I couldn't comprehend his reasons for unshackling himself from any contact with her in his new life of freedom.

As she and my father left the room together, that left Mom and me at the table. I spooned some Crunchy Nuts and milk into my mouth, interspersed with tablets given to me at hospital after my two ops. Mom had made me some tea just the ways us Okeys liked it; hot and sweet.

'What are your plans for today, love?' Mom said as she topped up her own coffee.

'Hair, tidy up in here then do some reading on the veranda. Oh ... and a half-marathon after lunch,' I joked.

Mom didn't laugh.

'Don't overdo it, Amber. That's what we're here for, your father and me. You can stay as long as you want. And having little Emma here, it's like a breath of fresh air. We might only be in our fifties but I've seen the difference in Barry already.'

I grinned. It was true. 'You're right there. He has a completely new audience for all those terrible jokes and puns that we've all heard loads of times. *Why did the chicken cross the road? For some 'fowl' reason.*' We exchanged a knowing smile. 'And then there's his dancing. He's no John Travolta, that's for sure.'

Mom came around to rest her hands on my shoulders, leaning over to kiss my cheeks. I could hear the emotion in her voice.

'My darling Amber. I am so sorry that all of this has happened to you.' She began to cry. I offered my napkin and she dabbed her cheeks.

I was a survivor. She'd taught me that. And I would get better.

'Look on the bright side, Mom. I have full sick pay for six months so I can sit around getting better without putting a money strain on you and Dad. It can't be easy running this farm — not with the drought and all.'

It had been one good thing to arise

from me being ill; financial independence. My job had not only been well paid but had had a brilliant medical care package. I'd been off work for five weeks so far and was damn sure that the buffer of over four more months would allow me the recuperation time I needed without rushing or stressing.

Mom stood up, repressing sniffles as she dried her eyes. 'Better get on with packing our special picnic hamper. Can't have your dad or Emma starving, can we?'

'She loves a yogurt, Mom. Banana ...'

'Just like when you were a kid. Dear Lord. Where did all those years go? Seems like yesterday you were fetching eggs with Barry.' She paused, staring at me as I nibbled some toast with peanut butter and jelly. 'Are you certain you'll be all right on your own?'

'Positive, Mom. Also, I will not be spending the time crying over Joshua. We're finished. I never want to hear from that stinking skunk again.'

⋆ ⋆ ⋆

Words define us all. In my case, they might have been 'mother' ... 'daughter' ... 'lover' ... though I was no longer a lover. Joshua had seen to that. Those words were simplistic and shrouded in preconceptions. Having this time off work had allowed me to see that I was often defined by my job title too, especially within my own mind.

Others judged us by those words, rightly or wrongly. When one of those terms changed, like 'healthy' to 'sick', our friends and family had to adjust — often as much as we did.

Yet we were more than words.

I was more than words.

I was still me ... but a different me. It would take time to allow that new woman to shine again.

And I would. I knew it in my soul.

If only it weren't so grindingly difficult.

Washing my hair was my main intention in the shower, though I did also use the time alone to shed some tears over what I'd lost. The trouble with breaking up is that, even though Joshua had hurt me deeply by making his attitudes obvious, I couldn't turn off my feelings for him as easily.

I felt better after that and dressed casually in a loose blouse and cut-off shorts that were a bit baggy around my waist. Threading a belt, I pulled it tight. The weight that I'd lost was unsettling.

No bikinis for you, Amber Devane ... not for a while, I thought after viewing the scar on my tummy. Still, I was alive — and that was more important than a line to spoil my skin.

Passing through the kitchen with my shades and a novel I'd recently bought, I decided to grab a packet of Kashi cookies from the cupboard and a beer from Dad's supply in the big fridge. Mom might disapprove of the beer in the morning, but hey. After what I'd been through, one beer to celebrate surviving relatively intact was justified.

It wouldn't affect the meds, most importantly.

Outside it was a typical Okey May day; blue skies and fluffy clouds with no sign of rain. Oklahoma could easily have five seasons in one day, tornado season being the fifth. The wild fires burning all over the state were a reminder of the constant need for rain to help soothe our sunburned countryside.

Scanning the horizon, there was never-ending sunshine. Another day in Paradise, some would say. My view was more pragmatic. After all, I studied weather; it was my job. Or had been.

When my dad was growing up, he told me that Oklahoma had droughts two out of every three years. Now, it was far more common. From 2010 through to 2015, we had experienced 239 weeks of continuous drought. There had been fires last year, and now this dry spell.

Despite what the government were saying, things were becoming worse. I was certain of it, as were my climate-expert colleagues. The only ones who thought otherwise probably still believed in the Easter Bunny and Santa Claus.

I sat in the shadow of the asphalt shingles that provided a sliver of shade all around my parents' homestead. A few black flies buzzed around but it wasn't yet summer so they weren't a problem. It was the perfect lazy day.

Kicking off my flip-flops, I stretched out on the sun-lounger with a table by my side. A few hours to relax and read and forget the past few nightmare months. The cookies would help; my favourite flavour, almond butter.

No sooner had I made myself comfy than I heard the pattering sound of Rusty's paws on the wooden decking. Our dark-brown Hangin' Tree Cowdog had a stick in his mouth and that unmistakable *Can we play?* expression in his plaintive eyes.

'Not today, old boy.' The thought of flinging even a stick made me shudder.

Rusty apparently decided he felt the same way. He was more than ten years old — a puppy when I'd left home for uni, yet he was a part of my childhood here and remembered me even now.

Noisily he slurped water from his nearby bowl, gobbled up some stray kibbles and then flopped down at my side, his eyes closing almost instantly. I gazed out at the dusty ranchlands and dead grasses, saddened by the sight.

After an hour of reading and demolishing the cookies, I felt my eyelids begin to get heavy. All right. The Bud hadn't helped. I popped a bookmark between the pages and set it to one side. It was cloud-watching time, a pastime taught to me by my mom and now being enjoyed by Emma too.

Looking skyward, there was an upside-down racoon floating by … followed by a white cat's face with pointy ears … and then …

I awoke with a start, automatically checking my watch. It took a moment to adjust and realise where I was and when. Rusty was lying watching me. It was ten past two. I'd been asleep more than two hours. Obviously, I'd needed it.

But something had awoken me. I heard a car door slam. It was far too early for the picnic squad to have returned. The plan was to give me some time off from my lovely but sometimes full-on daughter. Dad wouldn't bring them back until half-past five-ish.

I sat up, realising my hair was a mess. Also, my shirt was partially undone. Darn it. Mom hadn't been expecting anyone; she'd have warned me.

Mailman? Unlikely. Then who?

The answer wasn't long in coming. The crunch of shoes on the gravel around the corner changed to steps echoing on the decking; measured steps indicating a guy who wasn't in a hurry.

He turned the corner and stopped, staring at me; a tall, raven-haired man, dressed casually in a leather Stetson hat and aviator shades. As Rusty ran up to meet him, he put down the box of groceries he'd been carrying then knelt and ruffled the dog's fur. Rusty licked his hand. They were clearly friends.

'Howdy, y'all,' I greeted him.

'Is that you, Amber? Howdy, too. Didn't expect you to be out of hospital yet.' Hoisting the box into his arms he came towards me, Rusty padding along by his side.

I ignored the question. 'Barry and Rhonda are out. Can I help? ...Whoever you are.'

Placing the heavy box on a bench against the house wall, he stopped a few yards away, took off his hat and glasses and studied me, intently. I felt strangely vulnerable, wondering if anything were showing that shouldn't be.

'You don't recognise me, do you? So much for our friendship in college.'

There was something familiar about him; his intense brown eyes perhaps, though I couldn't place him. Then he swept a hand through his thick, wavy hair.

'Ryan? Ryan Crayson. Good heavens. You've changed.'

I couldn't believe it. When I'd last seen him at the college prom, he'd been a good bit shorter than me and thirty pounds heavier than he was now. Then I noticed that the glasses, which had earned him his nickname of Chief Four-Eyes, were absent. Ryan was part Cherokee and very proud of it, although it wasn't apparent at first glance.

He grinned, his teeth a line of white against his deeply tanned skin.

'Late developer plus contacts. Must say you've changed, too. No offence, but you look a bit dauncey.'

'And you still have a face that's double coyote ugly,' I retorted. We laughed, which was a big mistake for me. I doubled up in agony.

'Sorry, kiddo. No more jokes,' he said, with a very concerned voice. 'It is great to see you again. Shame it couldn't be under better circumstances. I gather you've had a rough time of it, Amber.'

'Yeah,' I replied, staring blankly at the horizon. It was evident he was fully aware of my tragic history. I finished off the lukewarm can of beer and patted the seat near the sun lounger. Ryan sat down. He had lost weight, but was lean rather than muscular. Sports had never been his forte.

'How come you're here, visiting Mom and Dad? Groceries, no less.'

'Tarnation. The frozen stuff. Almost forgot. Excuse me a mo.'

I made a move to join him as he hurried inside, but my body thought better of it. It was so frustrating. He returned with an empty box soon after, resuming his seat by me.

'To answer your question, I help out on occasion. Bring supplies, too. My folks passed away and yours sort of took me under their wing. I have my meals here sometimes when I give your dad a hand with some of the two-man jobs. Since I get a great deal of spare time during the day and I just have an apartment in Drumright, coming here suits us all.'

'So what's with the shades?' I teased him.

'Contacts. Makes me much sexier when it comes to chatting up girls,' he joshed. 'At least that was the theory. Turns out that a nerd is still a nerd, with or without thick-rimmed glasses.'

There wasn't much I could say. Ryan had been one of the smartest guys at college, but that never endeared him to the others. He'd had an unusual hobby, too. Whereas the other guys were into X-Box games and the girls were into pop idols, Ryan had been enamoured with ... butterflies.

Yeah, butterflies. It wasn't a cool thing to be raving on about to anyone who'd listen, so he'd ended up as a loner.

He'd studied them with a passion, although he'd never stuck pins in them and displayed them on a wall like a wannabe big-game hunter.

Added to his modest height and those dreadful specs his Mom had insisted on him wearing, it had all led to bullying of a slightly tubby guy who found it hard to stand up for himself.

That had meant I had to stand up for him. More than one jock had felt my wrath and occasionally my fists. That earned me a reputation as a blue-eyed bruiser, being right up there with Ryan the nerd. We had made quite a pair.

'I never did thank you properly for looking out for me in school, Amber.' Ryan was suddenly serious.

'How do you propose to do that, Mr Crayson? Cash would be good. Or perhaps a new body?'

He leaned across. I expected a kiss on the lips but he chose a cheek instead. I realised I was disappointed.

'I always wanted to do that because I had a crush on you. I realise you liked me, but not in the same way, Amber. Funny how things were so intense back then. Little did we know what the fates had in store for us.'

'Yeah. Life's a bitch sometimes,' I replied, feeling sorry for my own situation, then realising that Ryan might well have had his problems too.

I realised with a jolt that I didn't have a clue about this guy sitting opposite. I mean, was he married? Did he have kids? A girlfriend? What was he doing with his life?

I supposed it was a case of ladies first.

'I have a daughter … Emma. She's four, almost five now.'

'So, I've heard. I'd love to meet her.' Ryan sounded genuine and that made me ponder again if he had kids of his own. 'Tell me about her.'

'I don't want to hold you up, Ryan. I imagine you have a job to go to. Family?'

'I have a job … a great one. Night shift, though. My days are my own and happily, I don't need much sleep. Five or six hours. That gives me time to do what I want — which, right now, is catching up with you, 'Killer'.'

My nickname from my frequent scraps with all the bullies I came across at college. I'd made a difference, I hoped, giving girls and guys their self-respect and lives back. There had been one girl, Carla. She'd got herself a reputation. It wasn't true. I'd stood up for her, decking the ringleader who had begun the rumours. It had caused a few problems with staff and my parents but, once they realised that I was acting for the greater good, my vigi-

22

lante actions were often overlooked.

It was only years later that I realised I'd been a bully too. Humiliating other people at college, even if it had been to protect other victims, wasn't the best aspect of Amber Devane's teenage years.

'A night shift? What exactly do you do, Mr Crayson?' He smiled. 'Do you recall telling me once that I should aim high — that the sky was the limit?'

I shrugged. 'No ... but I said many dumb things back then.'

'It wasn't dumb. It was inspiring. I'm an astronomer. At Mendenhall in Still-water.'

'Wow!' I exclaimed, genuinely impressed. The observatory was about an hour from T-Town and forty minutes from us. Most people hereabouts were familiar with its dome-shaped silhouette against the night sky.

'Hence the night-time job, I guess. What are you studying right now?'

'Some black holes in the Horsehead Nebula. There's a possibility that we've found a white hole too, but that is very hush-hush.'

Black holes, I recalled, were so powerful that they swallowed starlight and whole solar systems with their gravitational pull. For years there had been speculation that all of the stuff that disappeared might come out elsewhere in the Universe ... a white hole.

Ryan continued, 'It's intermittent but it's there. You won't tell, will you?'

I giggled, instantly regretting it as pain stabbed through me. When would I learn to respect my patched-up body?

'I've kept your secrets all these years, haven't I? And I'll guard this one too, with my l ...'

I stopped short of completing the sentence. After all, I'd almost lost my life on the operating table. My heart had stopped during the procedure. It was a humbling experience. I'd almost died at the tender age of twenty-eight. Emma, my parents, my profession ... It was difficult to accept that everything I had learned, all of my plans and love I had for the future, had been so close to being gone forever.

Joshua had already told me we were finished, and we were. Well and truly. At least my illness had shown me how shallow he really was and for that, I was pleased.

Ryan repeated some words.

'Sorry, Ryan. Daydreaming. Thinking about past mistakes. Not working gives you too much time to have regrets about past decisions. You were saying?'

I did my best to concentrate. It was hard, as my stomach was suddenly rumbling. It was past my usual lunchtime and woman did not live by Kashi Cookies alone.

'I was asking about your profession? Your parents never mentioned that. Lots about you and your daughter then your ...'

'You can say it, Ryan. Cancer.' It was amazing how reticent most people were to even mention the word, as though it might be catching.

'I was going to say, your marriage

break-up. But yeah, the cancer too.'

I was becoming defensive. Assuming too much. Time to move on.

'So, I'm a meteorologist in Galveston.'

'You study meteors? Gee willikers, Amber.'

I gave him a glare. 'You and my dad must share the same joke book, Mister. Even Emma understands what I do. Might not be able to pronounce it correctly but she tries. What's more, I should remind you that not many people are familiar with the expression 'gee willikers' any longer.'

He grinned. Some things never changed. Even when Ryan tried to fit in with us ordinary folks, he never quite got the expressions right.

'We do get on, your dad and I. Listen. We could chatter on all day and I'd love that but I'm so hungry I could wolf down half a steer. Got any grub we might share?'

Like my dear old dad, Ryan had always been a bit of a throwback when it came to slang.

'Yeah, me too. Mom reckons I should get back to eating properly too. Shall we go inside?'

Gallantly he offered to help me up but I was determined to stand on my own two feet. I almost stumbled under his watchful eye but managed it with only a modicum of loss to my dignity. It was then that I realised Ryan had deftly avoided answering my question about family. Or maybe he'd simply forgotten? No worries. It wasn't as though I was on the prowl for a new guy or anything.

'Fancy a late full breakfast? Sausages, eggs, bacon and mushrooms? Or some waffles?' He was into the cupboards as if he lived here.

'Sounds good. Leave the waffles, though,' I said, feeling better than I had earlier. I offered to help but was told to take it easy as I'd probably burn everything.

'You could crack us a couple of Buds, though. There's some light ones in the fridge. Put 'em in there earlier. I'm driving, even if you're not.'

I smiled. Two beers in one day? Whatever would my parents say?

Probably 'Go for it, girl'. I'm sure
they'd planned this chance encounter
today while they were out with Emma.

Or perhaps not. Ryan had seemed
genuinely surprised to find me here.

I obliged the chef, who thanked me as
he juggled all the cooking on the Aga.
He seemed quite adept at it — much
more so than Joshua had been. Thinking
about it, there wasn't much my ex was
good at.

'You staying here long, Amber?' he
called, the noise from the bacon and
sausages sizzling and the extractor hood
making conversation difficult.

I moved closer. Like a flash, he reposi-
tioned my chair so I could sit at his side.

'Reckon I'll be here a while, Ryan. Why?'

'What about your ex-husband? No
chance of reconciliation? Not that it's
any business of mine, of course.'

'We're finished. He's still in the apartment we were renting, as far as I know.
Don't care any more. And he's not my

28

ex. We were never married, thankfully.'

Ryan mused on that.

'Was your home in joint names, then?'

'No. Only mine.'

He stared at me, intently.

'What?' I asked Ryan before thumping my forehead with the heel of my hand. I swore, using a word Mom would definitely not approve of. Joshua could stop paying the rent, yet I'd continue to be liable. Water, gas, power, insurance? They were all in my name.

At least we had separate bank accounts. Some bills would be paid automatically from my bank but, with the chaos of my recent life, ordinary practicalities had taken on a very low priority.

'Looks like I'll need to send some emails later. The little rattlesnake. He must have realised.'

'I'll help you if you want. I'm not due in work until eight-ish. Barry and Rhonda won't mind me staying for my meal. Nothing to go home for, anyway.'

I thought about that. It was a virtual admission that he was living on his tod.

As for me, it had been almost a month since Josh and I had split up and I'd moved back here, being admitted to the local hospital immediately. All my medical notes had been forwarded from Galveston. I'd been the main breadwinner. Joshua would have to take over the lease or downsize.

Tough. Actions have consequences and telling me he wasn't prepared to care for me in the most distressing time of my life ... well. It served the scumbag right.

'You'll get all the bonds and deposits back, Amber.'

'Yeah. I can give some of it to Mom. The farm's struggling a little. Thanks for the financial advice, Ryan. Sometimes having a geek as a friend can be very useful.'

* * *

We were busy sharing more reminiscences when my parents and Emma arrived home from their day out. Emma was tired but intent on sharing tales of the day's adventures. Her initial shyness with Ryan soon dissipated as he revealed himself to be finely in tune with some childhood games she enjoyed. In truth, he was a big kid himself, teaching her some new drawing skills as he engaged wholeheartedly with her.

'He's a natural,' I told Mom, watching them play chutes and ladders. Emma was familiar with the alphabet and numbers up to forty. Anything over forty was always a million.

Mom and Dad completed making the bolognese that we'd prepared. Peeling mushrooms had been much more fun when I shared the chore with Ryan.

It was seven and Emma was ready to crash for the night. A quick bath and the promise that Ryan would read her favourite story had her dressed and in bed. I eavesdropped from the hall as Ryan made *Hungry Caterpillar* chomping noises while he read. She was asleep within minutes.

Ryan came with me to the kitchen,

announcing she was cuddled up for the night. I told him I was grateful for his intervention. You can only read the same story so often before you start to dread it.

'I enjoyed it. First time I'd read it. Quite interesting. Of course, I'd prefer Clive Cussler but there are a number of similarities,' he commented with a wink.

Dad's voice interrupted us. 'Hey, you two. Come out here. You too, Rhonda.'

'Dad. Ryan's just about to leave,' I protested.

'It's important, love. Quick. Before it disappears,' he called again.

We wandered out to the back, opening the screen door. Dad was staring intently at the hills towards Silver City. At first, none of us could see a thing out of place.

'Where?' said Mom.

'Up yonder, sweetheart.' He pointed. 'Have you ever seen anything like it?'

'Oh my,' Mom exclaimed, putting her fist to her mouth.

I was at a loss until I spotted the sky on the horizon. Instead of azure or light blue, it was a pale shade of green.

'What do you make of it, Amber? You're the weather expert.' Dad had turned to me.

'I... honestly don't have the foggiest. Wildfires? Some strange rainbow?'

I hated lying to them, yet at this moment, I thought it best to best to be circumspect. After all, it was probably more than thirty miles distant. Ryan had sufficient presence of mind to video it on my camera. I kicked myself for not doing the same. When I returned with my phone, there was only the faintest tinge of the green in a tiny section of the sky. It vanished within seconds.

'Well. That's that. Wonder if anyone else saw it?' My father sounded disappointed.

'I doubt it,' I said. 'We're pretty isolated. T-Town's in the opposite direction.'

Some minutes later, I accompanied Ryan out to his Jeep, parked out the front of the house on the gravel drive. He turned towards the house, checking that we were out of earshot.

'What was it, Amber? You're a bloody weather expert. Besides. I saw you cross your fingers when you lied to your parents.'

Whereas I'd hesitated to tell them, I chose to confide in my one-time friend.

'You remember that children's rhyme? *Red skies at night ... ?*'

'Yeah. *Red skies at night,*
Shepherd's delight,
Red skies in the morning,
Shepherd's house on fire.'

He gave me an apologetic half-grin.

'Trust you to stuff it up, Ryan. Well, there's another rhyme I made up when I first discovered what green skies can mean.' I began to recite it as we reached his car and he leaned against it.

'Green skies at night,
Humanity's plight,
Green skies in the morning,
Chaos and storming.'

He paled and swallowed.

'Not good news then, Amber.'

I took his hands in mine.

'No. Not good at all.'

34

2

Another Perfect Day

It wasn't a great night. Every time I turned, I was jolted from my sleep to a sudden realisation of pain. My bedroom was fortunately away from the others. At least my family didn't have to be woken by my stifled cries.

Life these days was a fine balance between 'putting up with it' and taking potentially addictive painkillers. If anything, I'd chosen the agony path. I'd seen what the alternative could lead to.

Lying awake in the intense darkness of the countryside, I was happy that the noises outside weren't traffic sounds or late-night revellers on their way home. A few crickets and an occasional owl were much more conducive to sleep. Also, I could gaze out through open drapes to the moonless night outside.

I wondered about Ryan, working with

the telescopes. We could be gazing at the same stars — a connection with countless parsecs and light-years between us.

'*Starlight, star bright* ... I began to recite as I did to Emma, before a cloud eclipsed the twinkling light. Did it have a green tinge to it? No, I decided. My imagination.

Yet the spell was broken. My mind fought against thinking of the strangely-hued sky of the previous evening but it was a losing battle. Had it been an optical illusion? I hoped so. The alternative was too frightening to consider.

Oklahoma had always been a state of extremes. Last year's record-breaking temperatures and fires had been so brutal, they'd scorched the arid earth leaving death and dark destruction in their wake. We'd been spared most of it around the ranch; not too many tinder-dry trees.

The world's climate was a giant engine — or more accurately a series of engines, the air above dipping to kiss the oceans briefly before dancing off high into the troposphere to catch a jet stream and descend again.

I was a top weather girl with NWS, the National Weather Service based in Maryland. My climate models were innovative and a great predictor of general weather systems across the continent.

But even in the early twenty-first century with all of the satellite and deep-sea sensors at our disposal, all we could do was make an educated guess as to the forecast.

We could never change it. Mother Nature taunted us with her tantrums and volatile whims, often deciding to give us a cyclone with a few hours warning or a tornado with minutes.

As for foretelling the weather, mankind had been fascinated with that since the days of stone clubs and sweeping out the family cave. Soothsayers had gazed at the animal entrails, Aristotle wrote a four-volume work on weather, Galileo invented the thermometer ... and now computer modelling. All this time we'd been trying to make sense of the inexplicable, just so most people these days would have an idea of what to wear tomorrow.

I turned on the bedside lamp in my old bedroom. Yes, there it was on the wall, just as it had been through my childhood and teenage years. That cheap Black Forest weather house, owned by my grandfather as a boy, was accurate in its own way; a little man in a raincoat or a woman in bright clothing would appear like magic, telling three generations of my family whether the forecast was rain or shine. Those two wooden figurines had taught me about predicting the weather long before I learned about aneroid barometers. In their case, it was as simple as a hair relaxing or contracting due to the humidity in the air.

I turned off the light, my face turned towards the weather house. The little lady was outside. Today would be sunny. It was the same as every other day for the past four months, the man in his raincoat doubtless wondering if he'd ever see the light of day again.

And just like me, the 'sunshine lady' would not have a man by her side.

★ ★ ★

The following morning was sunny and fine. What a surprise. Breakfast was over and I was brushing Emma's hair as she concentrated on an old jigsaw that Dad had discovered in the attic. He was planning on going down on the back forty with his latest toy, a big five-hundred horse Case STX Steiger tractor but had, for some reason, gone into town instead.

'Ow, Mommy. You're pulling my hair.'

'Sorry, kitten.' The hard, artesian water from the farm borehole stopped the shampoo lathering sufficiently.

'Maybe if you used mine? It worked a treat on you, Amber. That blonde hair of yours used to glisten in the sun. Nowadays ... I half-expect a buzzard to be using it as a nest. Why don't you take more care of your appearance?'

'What? For a man? Fat chance of that.'

I wasn't feeling all that great. Something I'd eaten yesterday clearly hadn't agreed with me.

Maybe the bacon? Too much, too soon, perhaps.

'Oh yeah. While we're on the subject of men, what about Ryan turning up like that? Coincidence ... or a scheming plan by someone with the initials RD?'

'Whose initials are RD, Mommy?' piped up Emma. Damn. She was getting too smart.

'I believe your Mommy meant me, chicken. My name's Rhonda Devane and Rhonda starts with an R. Rrrr. Rrr-ronda.' Mom tickled Emma under the chin before resuming our adult 'discussion'.

'No, I didn't have any idea he was coming. In any case, I don't believe that Ryan is interested in you, not in a romantic way. He lost his wife and baby years ago. Never really gotten over it.'

That was a shock. I stopped brushing my daughter's hair.

'I didn't know. By lost, you mean she d-i-e-d?'

Mom nodded.

'He never said.'

'He wouldn't. It devastated him. He doted on her. They were never apart, even at work. Took us months to get him to take an interest in anything again. He's quite sensitive and fragile.'

That was true. I remembered how he'd been at college. There had been a vulnerability in him back then, suggesting he was uncomfortable about his talent with maths and physics. I felt so sorry for him now, and his dreadful loss.

My own problems were nothing compared to him losing the love of his life. Joshua had never been that for me. Sure, I'd loved him — but it was not heart-wrenchingly intense.

Dad entered the room, panting. He'd been for some more cattle feed. There wasn't much out there in the fields for them to munch on.

'I met old Bill Grover down at the feed shop. He saw those funny-coloured skies too last night. His cattle, too. Spooked them, good and proper.'

'Cattle?' I said, immediately. 'But they're colourblind.' The adage about bulls seeing the red cape waving around in those Spanish bullfights? It was never the colour but the movement.

'Exactly,' Dad explained. 'There was something else up there above them. Maybe magnetism, electricity in the air. Animals have different senses to us sometimes; like migratory birds using the magnetic field around the Earth to navigate. Either that, or aliens searching for their missing flying saucer at Area 51.'

Everyone turned to me as the expert. I felt like the turkey asking what everyone was having for Thanksgiving dinner.

'It's possible. Any word of lightning strikes?'

Dad was disappointed.

'Not that I've heard, love. I'll call around. What does it mean? Are we going to get rain at last?'

Again with the crossed fingers. 'Maybe a little.'

It was then that I noticed Emma with

eyes wide-open and that fear in her face.

'I don't like lightning, Mommy.'

She was almost whimpering. I shouldn't have mentioned it near her. It was time for some serious mother-daughter time to calm her down.

As for contacting my workplace in Galveston, I'd do it later ... but out of anyone's hearing.

* * *

Dad interrupted our game of Kerplunk about an hour later. I apologised to Emma, suggesting that she do some colouring in by herself, which she was happy to do. Then I followed Dad outside.

'Didn't want to upset Emma any more with talk of lightning, Amber, but I rung around and there was a whole bunch of strikes out Silver City way, right under them weird skies. They did something real funny with the sandy soil over there.'

'Let me guess. Turned it into glass.'

'How did you ... oh, you seen this before?'

'No, Dad. But I've heard of them. Fulgurites. Lightning fuses the sand to make beautiful shapes, but they're very fragile.'

Dad scoffed.

'Not these ones, precious. They're so hard, they broke Pedro's hammer when he tried to smash them. They're all over the field where his cows are. Lucky none of them were zapped too.'

'Dad,' I ventured, feeling a wave of excitement re-energise my body. 'Any chance you can take me out there? Emma too? I'd like her to see these fulgurites.'

'You can drive yourself ... Oops. Sorry. I forgot.' Turning a steering wheel or changing gears wasn't possible for me for a while. 'There's no problem taking you. Reckon Rhonda would fancy a looky-see too.'

'Thanks, Dad. I'll go get us ready. One other thing. Can you give Ryan a bell, explain where we're going and ask him to meet us there? And before you ask, that's because of his expertise, not because I fancy him rotten ... Which I don't.'

Darn it. What had made me say that? Dad had walked away, so no harm done. I trusted him to keep it to himself.

★ ★ ★

Sitting on the back seat of Dad's Chevy Impala wasn't that comfortable. I flinched at every jolt as we made our way towards Silver City. Emma reached over to take my hand, showing her concern. Finally, I'd had enough and asked him to pull over for a sec while I rummaged through my handbag for some Tramadol.

I couldn't find them and was becoming agitated when Mom handed me a pack she'd thought to bring for me, from the supply in the secure bathroom cupboard. I took one — then, on reflection, a second — washing them down with a few swigs of water from my bottle.

'Are you certain that you're up to this, darling?' she said, showing her maternal concern.

'Okie-dokie,' I replied bravely. 'I need to do this. It's my job.'

'Was your job, Amber. You're on sick leave in case you'd forgotten.' Mom was trying her best to care for me, but she, of all people, understood that there are times you put others before your own well-being. She'd been a nurse for three decades, taking leave for the present having offered to look after us.

'I won't be doing much, just taking a few photos to send to my boss. It's important, Mom.'

She conceded defeat in the argument but, being the same temperament as me, she had to have the last word.

'When we get back and have lunch, it's back to bed for you this afternoon. Y'all understand?'

'Yeah. OK.' I probably would have done that anyway. This trip was shaping up to take its toll on my body. Plus, I had a check-up back at the hospital tomorrow. I didn't fancy another lecture from Mr Calinich as well.

I sat back and closed my eyes, loosely holding Emma's hand. The landscape outside was so depressing. Dust devils swirled around much more frequently than I remembered from my childhood and despite it being spring, no welcome rains were in sight.

Just as I was dozing off in the cool of the air-con, the car lurched violently, flinging me against the door panel. I groaned loudly. Something had dug into my side where one lot of stitches were. Almost as suddenly we were out of whatever had hit us, Dad slewed the car to a stop on the Tarmac.

'Everyone all right? Amber? Damned if I've seen anything like that in my whole life.'

'What was it, Barry?' Mom asked, turning in her seat to see my teeth clenched together. I lifted my blouse awkwardly for her to view the incision. The stitches were intact.

'Dust-devil. She's coming back for

us.' Dad nodded towards the side window and I forced myself to open my eyes more to check out the mini twister.

'Whoa. Get a move on, Dad.'

I couldn't believe it. Instead of the playful whirlwinds I was used to, this was a solid cone of dirt and debris over one hundred feet high. We'd been lucky it hadn't flipped us the first time; I didn't want to try it again.

As he gunned the engine and straightened the car, I twisted my head to gaze back. The twister vanished as I watched, the suspended particles drifting to the ground like flakes in a snow-globe.

* * *

The rest of our journey was thankfully less eventful. Nonetheless, I was wide awake once more, the pain decreasing to a manageable level.

Emma hadn't been concerned at first, thinking the car spinning to be fun. She was astute enough to pick up on our concern, though. Great. Another thing to scare her. As if life wasn't difficult enough for her already.

I'd brought Emma to see the 'frozen lightning' in the hope that it would give her a more calming association than an unnerving flash and thunder.

As we pulled up in the yard of Dad's friend, I noticed Ryan's old Jeep. He was here.

He approached our car, dressed casually in hat, shorts and boots. It was functional but hardly haute couture. The long khaki socks completed the strange cowboy ensemble. The moment she could, Emma dashed over to give him a welcome kiss. He knelt down to hug her.

'We seened a dust-devil, Ryan. It was scary,' she told him.

He stood up. 'Scary?'

Dad explained, finishing with, 'Bad news, Ryan. Weather's going crazy.'

We met up with Dad's friend Pedro and his wife. Pedro was about sixty, a typical rancher with wizened skin the colour of an orange. His wife, Carlotta, was matronly with her hair in a bun. She fussed over Emma, making her feel at home. I made certain that Emma had her little hat and shades on, like me, as we headed out the back of the sprawling ranch house and machinery sheds.

'You two are scientists, are you?' Pedro asked Ryan and me. Emma was in between us, holding our hands. She wanted to swing but I had to tell her no. I didn't have the strength.

'Yes,' Ryan replied. 'I'm an astrophysicist at Stillwater and Amber here studies weather. She's based in Galveston.'

'Long way from Texas, lady. Hope you can make sense of all of this. The wife filmed it all on her cell phone. We can have a look at that, after. Daisy almost got barbecued with one of them bolts from the blue. Certainly scared her something awful. No milk today.' He pointed. 'There, just over there behind them trees.'

It was then that I spied an older man waiting in the shadows. He wore a breechcloth, leggings and the traditional moccasins of the Cherokee. His long white hair was plaited on both sides and his weathered skin was adorned with tattoo art. Although he was elderly, his eyes shone with a mischievous child-like quality.

'Howdy, Barry ... Rhonda. Good to see you again.' He came to shake all our hands. 'You two lovely girls must be Emma and Amber. I'm Salal's grandfather; Chea Sequah or Red Bird in English. You can call me Red.'

Emma was fascinated by him and his clothing. Also, his hair, which mirrored the way her gran had tied hers today.

'Red Bird?' I said. 'What? Like a cardinal?'

'Exactly,' he replied. 'Have to admit, you're a lot prettier than Salal told me.'

'Salal means what, Red?' I asked. I realised that it was his pet name for Ryan.

'Oh, that. It means squirrel. Ryan here has always been a little nuts,' he joked, his dark eyes sparkling in the shade of the trees.

'Ignore him, Amber. Actually, it was because I loved pecan nuts as a kid.'

51

'Couldn't get enough of them,' his grandfather agreed, clapping Ryan's shoulder. 'Now, let's see what the Thunder Boys have been up to. Carlotta? Pedro?'

We made our way through the gate to an open field surrounded by more trees. There were a dozen or so cattle, presumably including Daisy, grazing on the pasture irrigated from the stream running down one side. I guessed it must be artesian as most streams and rivers had long-since dried up.

Then we noticed the fulgurites. We five visitors stood there in shock. Rather than lying on the sandy soil, they were sticking out of it, some almost three feet high. Furthermore, they were green – as green as the grass in which they nestled.

'Wow. They're fantastical, Mommy.' Emma was first to speak. She was staring at the closest one, now illuminated in its verdant beauty as the sun moved from behind a cloud. Soon the others shone too, the myriad facets of the glass twinkling like Christmas trees. There were eight of them, neatly arranged in a circle.

'Well, I'll be danged,' Dad added.

I'd never seen a crop circle – yet to see these, arranged so symmetrically, was almost as unbelievable. I fumbled in my bag again. As I raised my camera to my eyes, I caught sight of Ryan panning the area with his cell phone.

'Dad. Will you take over, please? I want a comprehensive record of it all, up-close shots. Everything. Try to include other things to show scale — how large they are.'

'Sure, Amber,' he replied, taking the camera from me. 'What will you be doing?'

'I need to advise my boss in Galveston what's happening. Right away.'

* * *

At first, the Prof's assistant, Brenda-Lee, explained that he was in a meeting and couldn't be disturbed.

I'd told her to pass on a message, urgently.

Two Latin words. *Viridi aetheres*. I'd spelled it out. Professor Chuck Polanski returned my call three minutes later.

'Amber. What's going on? You're off sick.' His voice was gruff but then again, it always was.

'I'm in Tulsa with my parents. I've sent some photos and … ' I turned to Ryan, who had just entered my boss's email details onto his cell phone. He nodded at my unspoken question. 'And video. We had a Green Sky incident last night. Home video of that to follow. We're at the field now. Fulgurites. Just as we predicted.'

'You predicted, Amber. The Viridi Aetheres Hypothesis was all your work.'

It was Latin for green skies, an idea that I'd proposed two years ago. Apart from presenting it in person, there had been a paper that was published worldwide in journals that covered weather predictions and climate behaviour. Like all such ideas, it was theoretical and — until now — had been just an unproven concept. I waited breathlessly as he viewed the photos and Ryan's video.

'I'll be up there with a team in … about two hours. I'll also contact the local sheriff to secure the area. We don't want souvenir hunters trying to steal the fulgurites, do we?'

I hadn't thought of that. I wondered if Pedro had told anyone else or if Carlotta had posted her video of the green skies overhead on Facebook. I asked them. The answer was no.

Ryan came over to my side. He'd brought me a garden chair, complete with cushion. Gratefully I sank down into it.

'Listen, Chuck. I can't be involved in this.' I heard his exclamation of surprise. 'Quite frankly, I'm not well. I came out of hospital two days ago and have no intention of returning there any time soon.'

Moving the phone away from my ear as he protested and argued, I sighed, waiting until he'd finished.

'Chuck. You have the address and my report. I won't be here when you arrive. Now, please … leave me alone.'

I hung up and turned my cell off. Smiling weakly up at Ryan, I attempted to explain.

'The Prof is one of those people who thinks the world revolves around our jobs. To him, this is ground-breaking, a vindication of my theories about this new weather pattern. He can't accept that I refuse to be a part of this.'

'I'll protect you,' Ryan offered gently.

'Thanks, Ryan. But I don't need protection from you … or my parents. I need people to understand and give me my space to get better in my own way. I want to be the woman I was until a few months ago – fearless, confident — hell, even a pain in the rear end at times. Right now, I feel … I don't know … broken. No amount of other people covering me with Araldite is going to repair Amber Devane. I have to heal myself.'

I stood up, again having to steady myself on the arm of the chair.

'Right now, I'm intending to teach Emma about fulgurites and lightning and then I'm going home. It's been a long day.'

It wasn't yet midday.

*   *   *

I did spend some time introducing my lovely daughter to the fascinating fulgurites. As Pedro had said, they were solid and heavy. Although some that had apparently been discovered by Charles Darwin were longer than thirty feet, these ones were still impressive. A lightning strike might carry one hundred million volts of electricity.

By the time I'd finished, the sheriff had arrived. We were all invited for lunch by Pedro and Carlotta and although I had to decline, I urged the others to stay. Ryan, who had other places to be in the afternoon, kindly offered to be my chauffeur.

The drive back was uneventful, neither of us saying much. For that, I was grateful. I was done in. It was frustrating to feel as I did, yet I suspected I had stressed myself over the weather thingy.

Once back at my parents', I grabbed a bagel and a glass of juice, apologising to Ryan as I left him to do his own lunch. I took mine to my bedroom where I crashed out on the bed. I was asleep before I had a bite.

Later, I must have stirred. Ryan was still there. He was arguing, presumably on the phone, as his was the only voice audible. I heard him say 'leave her alone', followed by silence. Then I was asleep once more.

★ ★ ★

When I did awaken and saw my untouched lunch still covered, I felt guilty at my earlier rudeness to everyone, but especially to Ryan.

It was only as I left the room that I noticed the sunny lady in the weather house. She had retreated to the doorway on her side of the bijou house. The black-garbed man was visible on his side, umbrella already up. There was a weather change coming. I prayed it wouldn't be as bad as I feared.

Out in the family room, it was late. My parents were reading quietly, and Emma was colouring.

'Ah. Sleeping Beauty awakes. Was it Prince Charming on his white charger giving you a kiss, methinks?' Dad wondered aloud as Emma came to hug me.

'Sleeping Beauty? Hah! More like one of the ugly sisters, Dad. What's the time, please?'

'Late, Amber. Seven o'clock. I've fed Miss Hungry Horse here. Cheese and salad. We were waiting for you before we had ours.'

I rubbed my eyes. Seven? I made a mental note to discuss my tiredness with Mr Calinich tomorrow. This degree of lethargy couldn't be natural — even though he had warned me.

'Did the Professor and his team turn up before you left the farm?' I asked, sinking down carefully on the couch. Emma snuggled up to me, wary of touching any delicate bits.

'He did, Amber,' Mom replied.

'Goodness. How can you work for such a grouch?'

'His bite is worse than his bark, Mom.' Whoops! That didn't sound right. 'And did he compensate Pedro and Carlotta?'

I guessed he'd want to take the fulgurites, as well as their recordings of the Green Skies Event.

Mom seemed happy.

'Oh yes. He did that. They were more than pleased with his offer. Carlotta was talking about updating their car but Pedro had other plans. I'm certain that they'll work it out.

'Carlotta was quite concerned about you, though. Thought you seemed a bit like a z-o-m-b-i-e.' She nodded towards my daughter as she spelled out the word.

'Granny. You do realise that when I learn to spell big words proper, I'll understand what you're hiding from me?' Everyone stared. Where had that come from? I had no idea Emma could reason so well.

'She just means that Mommy looks a bit pale, my poppet,' Dad cut in before anyone else could react.

'Oh. Pale, like white? Yes. She does a bit. Not her proper colour at all.'

Emma was so grown up at times, I was concerned she'd matured far too quickly. She was my little girl, and a part of me wanted to cherish that innocence for as long as I could.

* * *

Ryan had been adamant that he could easily give me a lift to the Tulsa Surgical Hospital and do some errands nearby. All I needed to do was phone him when I was ready to return home.

He collected me at eleven the following day, insisting that he'd had as much sleep after finishing the night shift as he'd needed.

To be fair, he always appeared great. Casual, yet quietly rugged and in control. He didn't rush or get irritated, but appeared to be one step ahead of me in his thinking as though he was the consummate planner. It was a far cry from the awkward boy I'd known at college, the one I'd felt sorry for all those years ago.

I was conscious of how much time we'd spent in one another's company during the past few days. Even Emma had commented on it. At this moment we were together again, with Ryan seemingly having nothing better to do with his spare time than ferry me from one place to another.

I offered to at least pay him for gas. That was a mistake. He reacted, if not angrily, then brusquely.

'Amber. I don't want your money. I'm quite well off financially, if you must know.'

'Then why?' I asked him. He glanced over to me briefly as he negotiated a bend.

'I could say it's my way of payback for all those years of your parents' kindness after Kirsten died, but that would be wrong of me. The truth is, I like you. I always did. Maybe it was a schoolboy crush back then but now ... I was kinda hoping for something more.'

I was shocked by his confession. In the close confines of his car, it made me uncomfortable, more so than I'd been.

'Ryan. I've just broken up with my long-term partner, Emma's dad. I'm recovering from an operation to remove parts of me riddled with a cancer that appeared from nowhere. My life has been turned upside down. This is not a good time for me to fall in love with any-one — I'm sorry.'

I began to feel queasy. Surely not car sickness; I'd grown out of that, decades ago. Dad had fitted a static strap to our car back then. It had helped.

'Amber. I do understand grief. You've lost someone you love, just as I did. The circumstances are different but the feel-ings are the same, especially the anger. I'm simply trying to be a friend. I never said anything about love.'

He was right. I had.

Then my stomach heaved.

'Ryan. Pull over! Going to be sick.'

'Sick bag, side pocket, next to you.'

I grabbed for it, just in time.

Ryan passed me a bunch of tissues and a bottle of water as he delicately took the bag, sealed it and walked to a trash bin on the suburban street. By the time he'd returned, I'd cleaned myself up. He took the tissues away too, having given me a disinfectant hand wash and made sure I'd sipped water to clear the taste.

When I felt well enough, I faced him, expecting to see revulsion in his eyes. There was none; only concern.

'You carry a sick bag?' I asked.

He shrugged his shoulders. 'I was a boy Scout. You're not well, Amber. What more can I say?'

As I thought. Ryan was prepared.

'Thanks, Ryan. I'd offer to kiss you but ...'

'Maybe later. When you're ready. I won't rush you.'

I'd meant a 'thank you' kiss on the cheek. I wouldn't have, anyway — not at that time — for obvious reasons. As for Ryan, he clearly wanted more.

We sat back in the car. I'd given Ryan

some reasons for my reticence over becoming romantically involved but they weren't the main ones. In truth, I was over Joshua. The minute he'd told me we were finished — in the hospital — I'd felt a wave of inner relief. Whatever we'd had, had disappeared years before.

He'd ignored Emma, only doing the bare minimum as a father. Once I'd realised that, nothing could have repaired our relationship. We'd stayed together out of inertia rather than anything else.

No. My main concerns about going into another relationship were far more serious. To know that your heart stopped in the middle of an operation was a life-changing thing. The burns from the paddles were still visible on my chest; they were itchy, too. When I'd asked why it had happened, the in-depth medical analysis had been, 'It was one of those things.'

They didn't have the foggiest. It had apparently happened suddenly, without reason. The fact that I'd been in theatre was all that saved me; doctors who hadn't panicked, with the machines to restart my ticker close to hand.

What if it happened again? I guess that would be it for me. No more plans or dreams for the future, no chance of watching Emma grow into the beautiful, talented woman that I was certain she would become ...

Ryan had already lost one soulmate. If we did get together and something happened to me ...

No. It was best not to get his hopes up. Or mine.

'You OK, Amber?'

'Yes,' I replied. 'Thanks for dealing with that. You're a true friend.'

* * *

Ryan dropped me off at the surgical hospital where I'd arranged to see my consultant.

Dr Calinich began with the pleasantries, asking how I was managing. I informed him of my continued lethargy and sudden nausea on the way in. While

I was rabbiting on, he was doing checks, blood pressure, pulse, the state of my operation scars and bruising. Finally, as if I hadn't lost enough blood already, he decided to relieve me of some more.

'Could you do an ECG, please, doctor?'

I'd been getting myself worked up and my blood pressure was raised.

'Everything seems OK, Amber. Are you sure?'

'Humour me, please. There have been times when I don't feel my heart's behaving.'

The grey-haired surgeon stared into my face before checking the masses of notes forwarded from Galveston when I'd been transferred here.

'I see you have had such feelings before, Amber,' he read aloud in his slight Austrian accent. 'It was how they found the cancer so early. There were no symptoms, yet you were correct. You have an astute awareness of your body. Give me a few minutes to get the heart monitor. No — better still, you will come with me. It will be easier. Please put this gown on and bring your clothing and bag. We will go to Professor Allen's office in Cardiology.'

Although I'd met my consultant only a few times, we had a good rapport and I had literally trusted him with my life.

In the Professor's consulting room, he positioned me on the couch and wheeled the machine to my side. Once the sensors were placed according to their labels and colours, I lay back as he took his readings. He was just about to stop the trace when there was an urgent knock on the door. A nurse burst in.

'Please come, urgently, Doctor. We have multiple passengers from a flight coming in by ambulance. Three minutes. Some incident before they landed.'

My consultant reached the door before instructing the nurse to assist me in getting dressed. The trace was still running.

'I'll contact you tomorrow with the results, Amber. Sorry. Must go.'

From the sounds and bustling out in the corridor, it seemed like a real emergency. I cleaned myself up after the electrodes were removed, wondering what the squiggly lines on my ECG meant. Like most medicine, it was unintelligible to me. It was only when I'd donned my blouse and slacks that I thought to ask the nurse what had happened.

'A bunch of people passed out on the flight from Denver, just as they were flying through some strange cloud formation.'

I stopped buttoning my sleeves.

'Strange? How was it strange?'

'That's just it. Darnedest thing, Miss Devane. The cloud was green.'

3

And Now for Our Weathergirl

It began to rain the following morning; the sort of light but steady rain that felt gentle on the skin and soaked into the parched, arid ground of the area around Tulsa.

T-Town is our state's second-largest city, with its county having around 650,000 people. The State capital was OHC, Oklahoma City. Our forefathers didn't have much imagination for names.

I loved T-Town — and not simply because Gene Pitney had made it famous in his song *Twenty-Four Hours From Tulsa* way back in the Sixties. My dad had taken us all to see him performing when I'd been eleven. It was magical. The singer passed away in 2006 and it was as if a part of Tulsa had died with him.

Maybe it had been coincidence that I

ended up working in Galveston. There was a song about that town too, by Glen Campbell. I had been offered work simultaneously in Albuquerque, New Mexico but there wasn't a song about there. After all, what rhymes with Albuquerque? Turkey? Murky? And at least I could spell Galveston.

I sat watching the weather girl on the telly telling us it was raining. Maddy was a pretty redhead but, I guessed, not a meteorologist. In her case, she was adept in reading a teleprompter on the camera but probably didn't have a clue about the difference between a stratus cloud and an isobar. As far as I was concerned, her credibility wasn't enhanced by the skimpy mini-dress she wore.

'The rain appeared out of nowhere, folks. We had no inkling those sneaky little clouds were waiting up there to give us some welcome rain but boy, are we glad they were. Unusually, the showers are coming down everyplace for at least sixty miles all around T-Town. They don't appear to be moving away either.

71

It's like they are stuck there in the sky, right over us.'

I grinned, despite feeling rough after another bad night. *Stuck there in the sky*, indeed? It could be argued that Maddy was simply giving us viewers our half-hourly snippet of weather in terms everyone could understand. After all, if she'd been using words like cumulonimbus, some people's brains would have switched off immediately.

No. The telly stations needed their viewing figures to be high so that they could charge more for their ads. It was simple economics. Presenters like Maddy were, as Dad so eloquently called them, 'fluff-bunnies'. Nevertheless, he made a point of watching her every morning.

Emma ran up to me. 'Mommy. Granny and me are going outside in the rain. Is you coming?'

She and my mother were in their swim-suits. It had been a family tradition when I'd been growing up to do a rain dance after rain broke a long drought; not so much to summon showers as to thank the rain gods or goddesses up there.

Dad hurried to don his trunks and join them after a final glance at Maddy in her mini-dress.

'No, kitten,' I replied. 'But I'll come and watch you all having fun.'

★ ★ ★

It was all coming true; my model of the Green Skies Scenario. I'd proposed it to a symposium here in Tulsa of our country's most eminent meteorologists a couple of years earlier. Other weather people loved our tornadoes, apparently. They were welcome to them, to take home. Me, I hated them just as Emma hated lightning.

I'd popped in to visit Mom and Dad back then. Emma had been just a toddler. She'd changed so much in those two years but, I supposed, all children did.

Life on the ranch was much better than in our three-bed apartment in Texas. Plus, they talked funny down there and

I dreaded Emma picking up that drawl.

It had been great for me as a child growing up here, with one enormous back yard to explore, all the animals and adventures ... and let's not forget the rain dances. Maybe I should transfer up to Tulsa when I returned to work? I'd be closer to my parents ... to Ryan too.

Angrily, I pushed that thought away. He was a college friend; that was all.

Wandering onto the back veranda with my toast and a fresh glass of juice, I sat under the roof. Droplets of water were encroaching on the decking so I pushed my chair back. Emma was having great fun splashing in the puddles and frolicking around. Mom and Dad too. They joined hands and danced in a circle before Mom led them in a stylised Native American-type dance where they bent over, put their hands to their mouths and made peculiar whooping noises.

Rusty came up, put his head to one side and watched the bizarre spectacle in wonderment.

My mind drifted to the weather above. The paper I'd written on the Green Skies was quite detailed even if it was speculative. The singularity had only been documented twice before in history; once in medieval Yorkshire, England, and an account from the Mayan temples on the Yucatan Peninsula around the time of their decline in the tenth century.

Years of savage droughts had been followed by lightning strikes, inexplicable illnesses and steady rains. That pattern was being repeated here. Nevertheless this time it was, I believed, only a portent of disasters yet to come.

I'd spoken to my consultant this morning. He'd rung to tell me that the tests all indicated that I was on the mend. The ECG showed no abnormalities. It hadn't reassured me, though. There was another thing wrong inside me — and I was certain that it was my heart.

For the present, I could only accept his decision. There was nothing tangible to suggest otherwise. My 'feeling' wasn't going to convince him.

When I'd asked about yesterday's emergency with the plane, he'd been extremely forthcoming. It wasn't common knowledge, he'd said, but he was happy to chat, asking my views based on my weather expertise.

'Never seen anything like it, Amber. About thirty people passed out. Their blood chemistry ... electrolytes ... They were all over the place. Luckily, everyone has recovered without any apparent lasting effects. You're a meteorologist. Have you heard about green clouds?'

I'd paused. 'Yes. I'm ... a specialist on that, unfortunately. Bad news. You'll probably hear more about it on the telly from my boss. I think the green skies will be here for a while and we'll all be in for some seriously foul weather.'

'I did sneak a peek online. Green skies mean a bit of hail, don't they?'

I'd winced, glad he couldn't see my reaction over the phone. 'That's a little simplistic. It's more like inviting a lion into your family room because your children love cats, Doctor.'

'That bad?'

'Worse.'

'Seems as though the local hospitals are going to be busy. I'd best make preparations. How long?'

'Hard to say. The rains will be mild at first, like today. Then the storms will begin. Deluges, floods, lots and lots of lightning and winds. I'm guessing a week. After that, we're in the lap of the gods. It could peter out or it might become worse still. Might I suggest you arrange for all hospital staff to sleep over when the floods hit? There won't be much heading home between shifts.'

'Thanks, Amber. I hear what you're saying but perhaps these rain showers are all we'll get. Extreme weather, like you're predicting, sounds a little too ... extreme.'

* * *

That was it. Even a learned man such as the good doctor wouldn't believe my forecast of doom. He dealt in absolutes, not the ravings of a glorified fortune-teller. Essentially that's all I was; with computer banks instead of a crystal ball.

I thought back to a short story I'd read recently about Heracles growing up in ancient Greece. The weather had suddenly turned nasty and the soothsayer was in trouble.

'Fine and mild with the chance of a shower,' the village elder had repeated, sarcastically.

'What can I say, boss? I just read the intestines; I don't make the weather.'

'Soothsayer. Unless you get your act together, it won't be a goat's intestines we'll be using. It'll be yours.'

Meanwhile, Heracles (or Hercules if you liked the Roman name) was out there in the massive storm, dodging lightning bolts sent from Heaven by his father, Zeus.

When he'd walked away unscathed and the storm had finished, he'd laughed, then asked Zeus if they could play again the next day. And that was the end of the tale.

It had made me realise yet again that weather was indeed in the eye of the beholder. To a rancher like my father, these rains were life-giving. To a mother who wanted to take her kids to the park, the rain was a nuisance. To an elderly man, unable to fix the hole in his roof, it was a problem. It was all a matter of perspective.

* * *

After Emma and my parents had finished outside, they cleaned up and changed. There was mud everywhere. Mom insisted on bathing Emma, leaving me with my feet up, listening to the soothing pitter-patter on the roof and smelling the evocative scent of rain on the soil; 'petrichor'. The word had been first used fifty years ago by two Australian scientists to describe the sweet, musty odour given off by the release of bacteria and plant oils into the air. I loved that scent. Mom came from inside with a fresh drink for me and one for herself.

As she sat, I asked her what Emma was doing.

'Sound asleep after her morning exercise. Her idea. Dad's watching a movie. Thought it was high time you and I had a bit of a mother-daughter chat. If you feel up to it, Amber?'

'Sure. I'd like that.'

The rhythmic sound of the rain lulled us as we both sat, deep in thought. I broke the silence by thanking Mom for caring for Emma. She and Dad had been a godsend. I couldn't have coped by myself.

'Joshua emailed me this morning,' I continued. 'I threw him out of my apartment. Technically, the rental people did the throwing. He wasn't happy. Seems he had a girlfriend already moved in and said I was being unfair. I said, 'tough' and not to contact me again. 'Actions have consequences' was what I said.'

'Good for you.' Mom put her hand on mine. 'Goodness. You're cold. I'll fetch a sweater.'

She did. I wasn't feeling great so she

helped put it on me. I hated being so weak and dependent.

'Ryan might call later,' she continued. 'The road's Tarmac so no hassles with mud.'

Making sure I was facing the back garden instead of Mom, I commented, 'I told him not to. Things were getting ... awkward between us. I wanted some space, Mom.'

'Space? I don't understand you, Amber. Ryan's a lovely young man. He's kind, considerate —'

'Don't go on,' I replied irritably. 'I realise he has great qualities. It's me ... not him.'

'That sounds so clichéd. Straight out of a Harlequin romance.' We both giggled at that, the ice broken. A few minutes of silence ensued, as we and Rusty soaked up the relaxing, watery ambience.

'Do you mind if I ask something, Mom?'

'You can always ask, love. Can't promise an answer, though.'

'Ryan. What exactly happened with

his wife?'

My mother took her time answering. Bad memories for her too, I guess. They'd been friends with her, too.

'Kirsten? Car crash at night, in the rain. It appears the contractions started so she decided to drive herself to hospital. Went off the road on a bad bend. Killed on impact. The baby too.'

'Wasn't Ryan there?'

'She was three weeks early. He'd been in New Jersey, doing a lecture at Princetown University. He was devastated and blamed himself for years for not being there. To lose the baby was one thing, but Kirsten was the love of his life. They were devoted to one another. Neither had parents so I guess Barry and I were their surrogate ones. Does that answer your question?'

'Yeah. I suppose Thanks, M — '

From inside, the doorbell rang.

'Your dad will get it.'

I wondered if it were Ryan. Perhaps I'd been too harsh yesterday, as we were coming home. I felt different today.

Still rough, but more positive about the future. My heart was OK, and they'd caught the cancer early. Parts of me were missing but, with therapy, the prognosis was very positive.

We heard the front door open and Dad talking to some guy. Next thing he was leading him through the house.

'It's some visitors for you, Amber,' my father announced loudly before opening the screen door and ushering them outside to us.

It was my chief, Professor Polanski. Immediately, I felt my body tense and a shiver ran through me.

'Gordon Bennett, Amber. I had no idea you were this bad.'

'You should have seen the other woman,' I half-joked, annoyed that he was here. I didn't want to be reminded of work.

The shocked expression on his lined face was ephemeral. In seconds, his usual jovial smile was back. Mom brought a couple of chairs over for him and his driver, Suzie, a junior at our weather office in Galveston.

The Prof didn't drive and rarely travelled these days. I should have felt privileged that he'd deigned to visit here as a result of my report and the video of the sky. In fact, I'd been the selfish one passing it on to my superior because, fascinating as it was, I had realised it was too much for me to deal with.

'Can I assume that you didn't wish to see me at that couple's ranch the other day, Amber? Also, that you're not too keen on me being here, either? Your boyfriend warned me off seeing you, on the phone yesterday.'

'You always were good at realising the bleeding obvious, Chuck. And Ryan's not my boyfriend,' I replied, with a far-away stare at the yard.

Mom cleared her throat, suggesting that I didn't talk to my boss in such a manner. But he was used to my plain-speaking and I wasn't particularly in the mood for niceties.

'What you've found here vindicates your theories, Amber. There have been a number of other incidents which we've suppressed from the news media so far. I thought that you should be aware of them. That's why I'm here. It wasn't a pleasant drive here so if you're not interested, Suzie and I will head back to Tulsa before the road becomes impassable. I'm on some local talk show on television later on.'

Realising that I'd jumped to conclusions, I apologised for my rudeness and asked about the incidents. Also, his cryptic comment about the roads. All of the time, I was aware that Suzie and he were becoming more comfortable with my gaunt appearance. I'd lost just over eighteen pounds. Hell, the outline of my lower ribs was visible under my clothing.

'Where do I begin? They haven't been widespread or earth-shattering but they are unusual and do fit your 'early days' profile, Amber. Air pressure fluctuations far more rapid than usual, cold pockets with fifteen-degree drops in two minutes or less. And the winds.'

'What winds?' I asked.

The air had been still, nary a breath for hours.

'Exactly. No winds. The weather system has stalled. Yet winds go from high to low-pressure areas so there should be winds. It's basic physics.'

'Chuck. I always predicted the very unpredictability of the Green Skies. All of our assumptions about the weather are literally up in the air right now. They're driven by actions far above the Troposphere which governs 'normal' weather. The sky colour indicates that. It's like a mini Aurora.'

Few people in the United States had seen the Aurora Borealis or Northern Lights caused by the impact of solar winds on the Earth's magnetosphere.

I had … up in Alaska, one year. It had been beautiful; a light display more spectacular than anything I'd ever seen. The sky had been aglow with wondrous shimmering lights phasing through colours of the rainbow. It had captivated me for over an hour, dissipating at the whim of the goddess of the dawn after whom it was named.

Chuck and I continued to talk but, in the end, my mind was made up. I wouldn't be accompanying him and Susie to the television interview. He reluctantly admitted that he understood, thanking me for bringing the spectacle to his attention.

As he left, he promised not to bother me again. He did suggest that, as he'd be around for some time working with the Tulsa NWS offices, I could always contact him when, and if, I were ready.

★ ★ ★

Once he'd left, Dad came out with us to the veranda. Emma was apparently fast asleep, her teddy in her arms. As we all sat, Dad mentioned that Ryan had rung when the Prof had been here.

Whether it was my anxiety from being disturbed by Chuck, or something else, I reacted badly.

'What's he doing phoning me? I told him to back off yesterday. For a smart guy, you'd reckon he could take a hint. I've half a mind to phone him back and tell him what I think of being stalked.' Clenching my hands didn't help me to calm down. I began coughing. Mom rushed to fetch some water. She must have realised that stress on the stitches was a definite no-no.

Once my attack had ceased, she checked my pulse. 'Try not to get agitated, pumpkin.'

Dad wasn't as kind or concerned. 'I declare that, at times, you're not the caring person we brought up, Amber. What is wrong with you, girl? Did it ever occur to you that Ryan might be interested in our welfare, your Mom's and mine? He was looking in on us, long before you appeared on the scene, expecting our help.'

He was angry — angrier than he'd ever been with me. I was shocked, though glad that Emma wasn't here to witness this.

'Barry,' Mom remonstrated, gripping his arm.

'I'm sorry, Rhonda but it needed saying. There's obviously something else troubling our Amber. She's keeping it bottled up. I reckon it's making her push us and Ryan away.'

Mom moved back to stare at me. I couldn't look at either of their faces. Instead, I stared at my clasped hands on the table.

'Is this true, Amber?' she asked. There was no anger there in her voice, just apprehension.

I began to sob. I'd tried to protect them from the truth, thinking that I could handle it. Obviously, I couldn't. I'd been so focused on myself, wrapping a cocoon around my inner emotions. Dad reached over to embrace me. Mom too.

I rubbed my arm against my cheeks to dry the tears as I forced myself to tell them. A secret is only useful while no one suspects.

'Dad. You're right. I'm so sorry. There's ... something that happened during the op. I didn't want to tell you but that was misguided of me. And now,

I'm wondering if there's something else wrong inside this body.'

I went on to explain about my heart inexplicably stopping. I'd not told them prior to that. Then I tried my best to explain my trepidation and fear about the same thing occurring again.

They listened patiently, only interrupting for clarification on detail. In a way, it was cathartic to share this; a burden shared and all that.

'Amber,' Dad began when I'd finished. 'We're annoyed that you chose to try to deal with this all alone yet we do understand. Explains your treatment of Ryan too. We didn't like Joshua. Bloody redneck. He never came to visit with you and Emma. Last time we saw him was at Emma's christening and I don't think he spoke to us at all.

'Not that I'm trying to line you up with Ryan with everything else in your life, but I think you could do worse than confide your feelings to him. If nothing else, he'd listen.'

I agreed. 'I had decided to call and

have a word. Hearing him calling here just caught me at a bad moment. The Professor turning up and seeing me as I am was something I had wanted to avoid. Now I'll be the subject of office gossip and pity.'

At that moment, Emma wandered out in her slippers, teddy in one hand and rubbing her eyes with the other.

'Mommy. Teddy's hungry.'

I glanced at my watch. 'I reckon we all are, kitten. Let's go in for lunch. You coming, Mom and Dad?'

They helped me up before we headed inside.

Mom whispered about getting a second opinion about my anxieties. Apparently, she was quite close professionally to a cardiologist at her workplace. Useful to have connections.

* * *

The rain continued as heavy drizzle during the evening. I had spoken to Ryan, mainly to apologise for being such an idiot yesterday. With Emma snuggled up in bed, my parents and I watched my boss being interviewed by some hard-nosed Tulsa presenter. I wasn't optimistic about the outcome. The Prof was an intellectual who found it difficult to engage with more 'ordinary' people.

Chuck was dressed in a scruffy suit and tie. Whoever had done his make-up had made a right pig's ear of it. His cheeks glistened with rouge and along with the long, white Santa Claus beard, the initial impression was that he was a drunk.

The interviewer, some fellow called Lachlan, began with introductions before entering into what could only be described as badgering. What was all this about? My boss wasn't a killer or a CEO of some dodgy company polluting the environment. He wasn't even a politician.

'Professor. You asked to come on here to my show in order to warn the local populace about some dangers associated with the strange coloured skies some people have supposedly seen.' Lachlan fluffed his mauve cravat.

'Yes, I have, young man. The Green Skies are an indicator of dangerous weather patterns which could affect everyone around your county. Floods, lightning storms, freezing winds, huge tornadoes … these are all very real possibilities over the next few weeks. We should be prepared.'

Chuck was agitated and clearly hadn't been briefed on where to look to be on camera. He was speaking too quickly, glancing furtively around.

'You haven't been having too many nips of Southern Comfort, have you, Professor? I mean, Green Skies?' Lachlan preened.

'I have photos, you young whipper-snapper. Videos …' The Prof was becoming flustered. I sat forward on my cushioned seat, feeling a touch of dread at the interviewer's vicious tone.

'Photos can be faked. Videos too. I've seen CGI images of dinosaurs, Professor. Changing the colour of a photo? I can do that on my tablet. As for the weather? All we're seeing is some long-overdue showers. Sounds to me like you should change your name to Professor Chicken Little. Is the sky going to crash down on Tulsa, too?'

My boss didn't react too well to this irreverent and totally unjustified verbal attack.

'Lachlan, is it? I don't know what qualifications in science you have but I can only assume they are from the back of a Coco Pops packet. The area around here will suffer from extreme weather. My assistant has studied this situation carefully …'

'Your assistant? Let me guess. Some pretty woman. Where is she, this unnamed purveyor of Armageddon? Hiding from the non-existent thunder and lightning under her bed?'

If there had been an audience, I was certain the presenter would be expecting mocking laughter.

Chuck clearly felt very vulnerable now. He was out of his comfort zone and on the defensive.

'She is indisposed. That's why I'm here. The Green Skies are the result of the prolonged El Niño effect on the Pacific circula …'

'I'm sorry, Professor. That's all we have time for. We'll be right back after the ads with Tibbles, the cat who can sing. Don't go away now.'

Dad turned the sound off as we sat dumbfounded. Mom eventually spoke for us all.

'Your poor chief, Amber. I can't believe that Lachlan man ignored him.'

'Humiliated him, I'd say.' Dad was fuming. 'Or tried to. That was the most disgusting bit of … Amber? What's the matter?'

I sat there, angrier than I'd been for ages.

'I let Chuck down, Dad. Not just that. I'm convinced that these Green Skies will bring chaos and havoc to hundreds of thousands of people but now — despite the warnings — no one will believe it.'

4

The Kaleidoscope

It was the morning after the night before and, while I hadn't been drinking anything alcoholic, my mouth continued to taste like the tray from Tweety Pie's cage. I'd have to phone Chuck later, or maybe just text him.

There was no rain; not even a cloud in sight but I knew it was literally the calm before the storm. Tulsa was in for some horrendous weather even if that television presenter from last night stated otherwise. My daddy had told me a bit about him. His name was Lachlan Peabody and he was new to the station. It appeared that he was one of those obnoxious sorts that no one admitted to liking but everyone would happily watch. He'd built himself quite a following of enamoured fans; Lachlan's Lassies, he called them.

Getting up, I donned my house-coat and was about to head out to the kitchen for breakfast when I had a second thought. I wasn't the sort of woman to wander around for hours before getting dressed. No, siree. This lady was having a shower and getting dressed before facing her loving family. Afterwards, I figured on taking Emma for a mosey around the farm and maybe play some games with her; tic-tac-toe was a favourite at the present time. She liked to do the Xs rather than the Os.

I tossed my housecoat down on the ruffled bed and walked into the adjoining bathroom. Rainy Man was silently watching me from the Weather House on the wall. Sunny Lady was nowhere to be seen and, if my guess was right, she wouldn't be around for quite awhiles.

* * *

'Howdy, sleepyhead,' Daddy said as I came out. I'd made an effort, even some lipstick.

'Hi, y'all,' I replied, noticing one of Emma's latest masterpieces Blu-Tacked to the tiles. Realising I hadn't seen that one, I ambled over to check it out. Her stick figures were really improving and the proportions were more realistic.

She ran towards me. The hug was tentative, the kiss wonderfully sloppy.

'Are you better, Mommy?'

'A bit, kitten.' I pointed to the drawing of three people with what seemed to be Rusty by their side. From the triangle skirt on two of them, I guessed who they were.

The man, though. Was it Joshua?

'Who do we have here, Emma?' I asked kneeling down carefully to be by her side.

'That's you and me, Mommy ... and a horsey ... and Ryan,' she replied proudly.

Although I felt relief that it wasn't Josh, I wondered about Ryan, especially as he was in the middle holding both our hands.

'It's beautiful, my gorgeous, big girl,' I said, kissing her forehead.

'Cereal again, Amber?' Mom asked me, as she assisted me to stand. I was still weak. How I longed to be my old self once more.

'No thanks. Waffles and syrup today. I'll do them.'

As though remembering something, Mom folded her arms like she always did when I was in her bad books.

'Amber. I went to give Emma a cookie as a treat but that packet I'd bought of my favourite ones had vanished. Couldn't find them anywhere. Then lo and behold, there was an empty wrapper in the trash can outside. Don't figure you know anything about that, do you?'

'Me? Of course not, Mom. Must have been Rusty.' I gave Emma a wink. She grinned back.

'That's what I figured, too. Good thing I got me a secret stash, one that Rusty don't know about.' She produced a packet and gave one cookie to Emma, who accepted it with a grateful thank you. Mom then sealed the packet with a plastic clip and was about to put it into the cookie barrel, but had second thoughts.

'I figure I'd better hide this one some-wheres safe ... in case Rusty's watching and gets hungry again.'

She went to the larder with Emma to choose a hiding place. I could hear them snickering as I prepared my breakfast. They were ages. Finally, they emerged.

'Rusty will never find them there, Grandma.'

'He better not,' Mom replied, with a mock glare in my direction.

Dad stood up and stretched, putting the newspaper down on Great-Granny's Chippendale bureau in the corner.

'Y'all coming to check for eggs, Missy Emma? Them hens can't wait all day.'

'I is coming, Grandpa.' Emma rushed over to the back door to change her slippers for boots. She could manage quite well without help.

Mom and I watched as my dad and daughter made their way across the puddle-covered yard, Emma looking gorgeous in her pink My Little Pony rain boots. Not the most practical of colours in the mud, but she was so happy. She waved to us through the window.

My waffles and maple syrup ready, I sat down to enjoy my breakfast. The television was on and, as was often the case with breakfast shows, the weather was on every fifteen minutes.

Maddy was there in a different short skirt yet there was something about her behaviour which caught my attention.

'That rain spell didn't last nearly long enough, folks and ...' She glanced furtively around the studio. 'I shouldn't really be saying this because ...' Another pause. 'The official forecast is sunshine everywhere, but me ... I'm not so sure. Something out there is screwing around with our weather and I'm asking for any of you good citizens out yonder if you see or hear anything weird, contact me on my Twitter account —'

I noticed shouting in the background. Maddy was speaking but her mic wasn't working. The camera cut to the news presenter who was obviously unprepared to be on camera so soon. He looked sheepish, apologising for a technical fault before some pre-recorded clip began rolling.

I stared at Mom and she at me.

'Well. Don't that beat all?' she said. 'Wonder what that was all about?'

'Whatever it was, Mom, I figure Daddy's favourite fluff-bunny is in deep trouble right now.'

It sounded to me that she'd been trying to do the right thing by the good folks of Tulsa County but some no-good varmint had bushwhacked her.

I hardly had time to finish up before Dad and Emma returned. Taking their rain boots off at the back porch, I could see they were upset.

Mom started telling her husband about Maddy on the telly but stopped when she saw his face. 'What's up, out there, Daddy?' I enquired.

'The hens. Never seen nothing like it in all my born days.'

Emma was watching both of us, her face showing upset and that she was in agreement.

'They're all right, aren't they?' I wondered. He had over forty good layers.

'Yeah. Clucking away like there's no tomorrow.'

'Then what, Barry?' Mom joined in.

'No eggs. Not one goldarn egg. It's like they's all gone on strike. What are we going to tell our customers, Rhonda?'

'Nothing … We got enough for a day or two yonder in the pantry. Do you figure that any of the neighbours have had the same thing happen?'

That galvanised Dad into action.

'I'll phone Jimmy over at the Lone Star Ranch. He might be a goldarn Texan but Jimmy knows more about chickens than anyone, even that Colonel fella in the Bluegrass State.'

I grinned. My daddy had never taken to Kentucky Fried Chicken or Colonel Sanders. He preferred fried okra or Oklahoma cow fries. Aware of what cow fries were, I avoided them at all costs.

Dad went off to his office to call his friends. Mom and I tidied all of the dirty plates and such into the dishwasher. Emma helped as much as she could, collecting the unused cutlery and stacking it on the worktop which was almost as high as she was. I had my suspicions about the hens and once things were cleared, I took Emma's hand and went outside.

'Whatcha looking at, Mommy?' she asked after a minute of staring at the heavens.

'The sky, kitten. Trying to see if there's any green up there.'

Bless her precious heart. She tried to help, finally proclaiming with a flourish, 'Nope Mommy. Just plain old ordinary blue.'

She was right, of course, and, despite my suspicions about the devastating consequences of greenness pervading the air above, I was disappointed. What if all of my predictions were wrong? I prayed they would be — but the scientist in me knew the truth.

'What are you two ladies fixing to do today?' Mom asked, joining us outside.

Already we could see a mist as the rain from yesterday was being evaporated by an exceptionally warm sun. It was only spring. Nevertheless, yesterday's showers had given a brisk freshness to the land around; a glad-to-be-alive feel.

In the distance, there was the sound of cattle speaking their own special language. I wondered what they could have to talk about; the tasty grass by the fence, perhaps? It wasn't just the other man's grass that was always greener, cattle liked the fresh, verdant stuff too. Green … I shuddered a little.

'You okie-dokie, Mommy? You feel cold.' She'd been holding my hand.

'Fine, kitten.' What was more surprising? Her grown-up empathy for others or the fact that her Texan accent was being altered ever-so-slowly to that of a true Oklahoman? *Okie-dokie, I figure.* What gems would she begin adopting next?

I realised that I hadn't responded to my mother's question.

'Today, Mom? Nothing special. Hanging 'round here, I guess; shooting the breeze. You two?'

'Your father's taking his new toy over the south field, planting some more corn. As for me, off to chapel. We have a wedding; Billy-Joe Kaminshi.'

'Billy-Joe? But she's still a kid.' My forehead furrowed. I remembered babysitting her when I was in college.

'Old enough to find herself in the family way. Her daddy insisted she and her beau tie the knot.'

By 'insisted', I was sure Mom meant a good old T-Town shotgun wedding. Some things never changed.

★ ★ ★

Later, when my parents had gone their separate ways, I was helping Emma with her reading as we relaxed on the veranda. Mother-daughter time was so precious, especially now after the events of the past few months.

We were reading *Horton Hears A Who*. The old favourites were the best. Mom had bought her *The Gruffalo* and that was the next one to try. Emma already loved the cartoon.

We were so engrossed, neither of us heard Ryan behind us until he announced himself. 'How are my two favourite girls today?' I jumped.

'Lordy, Ryan. You almost gave me a heart attack.' That expression suddenly had a much more sinister connotation.

'Hey there, Amber. Not thinking. Sorry.'

'It's OK. No harm done, not really.' I decided that, like my parents, I needed to put him in the picture about everything. If he wanted to move on elsewhere, well ... who could blame him? I wasn't exactly pristine and, rightly or wrongly, taking on a woman with a child wasn't exactly most men's idea of an ideal relationship.

He dragged up a chair, ruffling Rusty's fur.

'I was just passing and figured I'd drop in.' It was a blatant lie. We were well off the beaten track. 'Your folks around, Amber?'

'Nope,' I replied, detecting the scent of Nautica Voyage. Nonchalantly, I fanned my face to dispel the smell. It had been Josh's favourite. He used to splash it on literally everywhere.

'Fair enough. Though they might have been interested in my special surprise too.' Emma clapped her little hands, joyfully. 'Get your glad-rags on you two. No. On second thoughts, you're both perfect like you are.'

'Are we going on a picnic, Ryan?' Emma inquired, her eyes as big as saucers.

'Yes. A very special picnic. I've already packed a basket.'

I wasn't happy. He was pushing me and one thing I hated was a man making decisions for me. 'What about me walking? I'm not strong en ...'

'Already sorted, my little Tootsie Roll. Don't worry your pretty head about it. Emma. Could you fetch your rain boots, please, and your shades? Oh, one other thing I forgot to bring. Some honey? You know, in the plastic jar, please. They'll love the honey.'

'Who will?' both Emma and I said, in unison.

Ryan tapped his nose. 'That's the surprise.' Despite my anger, I was intrigued. I was cheesed off at his assumptions though, and I couldn't quite suss out what was happening.

'Ryan — ' I began.

'Yeah, I realise. Too pushy by half. But this is too good to be missed.' He then explained where we were going and who the special friends were that we were going to see. I was on my feet in an instant, my eyes wide with absolute joy. I'd heard about these phenomena but to actually see one for real? Wild horses wouldn't keep me away.

The drive to the Keystone Ancient Forest didn't take long. It wasn't far from the Arkansas River and Keystone Lake. I'd forgotten how magnificent it was with its three-hundred-year-old oaks and five-hundred-year-old cedars. That was around the time Columbus 'discovered' America — of course the native Americans had been around long before ol' Chris.

Ryan had suffered loads of name-calling for his heritage after the Millenium back in the 'aughts'. People hereabouts hadn't moved on much, sadly. And these days were the twenties. Prejudice was prejudice whether you were Sioux, Hispanic, Jewish or even a woman. I prayed that Emma's future would see more tolerance of everyone.

I mentioned Maddy and this morning's television fiasco. Ryan hardly watched the morning news as he was generally asleep then.

'Has anything happened up at the observatory?' I asked him in between Emma's impatient 'Are we there yet?'s. Eventually, she would settle down. The scenery was stunning and Emma had already marvelled at the sight of some deer.

'You mean little green men in space-craft requesting an audience with our leader? Nope.'

I sniggered. The pain was more bearable today so I could afford to relax somewhat.

'Any comments from your co-workers? Funny weather? You're pretty high up there.' I gazed out through the trees to the morning sunshine glistening on the river.

'Afraid not. Like you said, it's early days. You heard about the sick folk on the plane from LA?'

'I thought it was Denver?' I said, facing him.

'There's been another. Bigger plane, more passengers affected. The theory is the body's chemistry is being screwed up by electromagnetism. The ionosphere is too low or something.'

'Oh. Hope they're all right.' I checked my watch. The second hand wasn't moving. Figuring it must need a new battery I asked Ryan if we had far to go.

He burst into a loud guffaw. 'I declare. You two are so alike. Impatient, you are. It's just around that bend … the parking lot, that is. Then it's a short walk … or roll in your case, Amber.'

Once we arrived, we had to line up. There were stacks of cars for a weekday. Word must have got around.

Unpacking the car, I felt uncomfortable at Ryan opening up the wheelchair. I could walk a bit but the opportunity to use it if I needed a seat was much appreciated. Like I figured, Ryan was a planner and he was caring for me.

'Your carriage awaits, Your Ladyship.'

Ryan bowed and then helped me settle in. He'd borrowed it, realising that I might have found it too difficult otherwise. I placed the picnic hamper on my lap. It was only then did I peer upwards at the imposing canopy of trees.

I squinted. 'Ryan. Does the sky look green to you?' To me, there was the barest hint of a pastel April green, the splash of colour on deciduous trees that heralded new leaves ready for the arrival of spring.

He gave a cursory glance then another longer one. 'Yeah. You're right, Amber.

112

Does that mean trouble?'

'No. But it might explain why they're here.'

As if to confirm it, tiny wings flew overhead.

* * *

It was strange at first, staring up at everyone apart from Emma. She loved it though, me being the same height as her, sort of.

'What are we's going to see, Ryan?' she asked as we set off with the other arrivals down the Frank Trail.

'A kaleidoscope, Missy Emma. Have you any idea what that is?' Ryan asked her.

'I seed one a few weeks ago, I think. Grandpa showed me when Mommy was in hostiple.'

She had indeed. Daddy's old playthings fascinated her. She'd apparently loved the changing patterns in the tube of glass and mirrors of the kaleidoscope he'd found.

113

'Well. We're going to see another type of kaleidoscope, Emma. One that's just as colourful, but this one's alive.'

It was then that we noticed the fluttering of tiny wings as some butterflies circled around us before heading down the track into the forest. Wherever they were going, so was everyone else, the buzz of their own excited voices lifting the occasion from the mundane to the extra-special.

I decided that I should try to walk, as the wheelchair made it too difficult to turn and witness the cavalcade of colours now swirling around us. Plus, it wasn't a flat path and Ryan would soon find it difficult pushing me up slopes. He was no athlete, that much hadn't changed.

Ryan's love of butterflies had prompted him to bring us here to share that joy. Thoughts of Green Skies and extreme weather vanished from my mind. If what he'd told me back home was correct, this was set to be a once in a lifetime experience for all of us.

Then the signs appeared. No collect-

114

ing of our friends please. It made sense. Orange-garbed volunteers were there to police this simple rule, and to share their knowledge with eager listeners.

Emma was so excited. Like us all, she could sense the wonder. A couple, total strangers, came up by our side, their smiles so infectious.

'The Kaleidoscope, man. Everyone's coming to see them. We're just on the edge of it now but even here, there are so many of them. I can hardly wait to see the Nexus.'

The Kaleidoscope? A collective name for a gathering of butterflies. Suddenly, a group of seven alighted on my bare arm and I could almost feel their energies flowing into me. Then I stumbled on the uneven surface. The teenage girl caught me. 'Are you sure you're OK, lady?' the pretty blonde asked. 'You look really pallid.'

'My mommy's been sick,' Emma explained.

I thanked her for her concern. 'It'll be all right now that I'm here, thanks.'

I stopped as the insects flew so close, I was able to hear the wispy flitter of their wings. After more reassurances that I was fine, the youthful couple wandered off, entranced by the cloud of colours that surrounded us all.

Apparently, we were within a space that was now alive with the butterflies. Alongside us walked people of all shapes and sizes, determined to experience a little of this enchanted wonderland.

'Get your commemorative T-shirts here!' one hawker called out from his hastily built booth on the side of the track. I looked around. Considering it had only just begun today, the enterprising park rangers had done some pretty quick-smart organising. There were butterfly ice-creams and hats, plastic wings for the children, costumes, mugs; all alongside the well-trodden pathway to the centre of the Kaleidoscope. In another situation these tatty stalls would have cheapened the occasion, however in this instance they only served as an overture to something remarkable.

Everyone was laughing happily, a few were singing songs and we weren't even there as yet. A balmy wind caressed us as we followed the pathway on this warm spring morn.

'How was it? The Nexus?' an elderly man with a walking stick asked a teenage girl as he passed her going the other way.

'Fantastic. I've never seen anything as beautiful in my life,' she replied as she skipped along.

One minute, the heavens were dotted with the tiny insects, along with a few cotton-wool clouds. The next step and we were there. The sky above was now pulsing with flickering rainbow wings. There were so many, the skies above were hardly visible and although one would think that it would be dark, it wasn't. The sight caused us to stop and stare in astonishment.

'Wow!' Emma exclaimed. 'Big wow.' She was speaking for us all.

'I know,' a pretty young red-haired stranger on my right agreed. 'Do you folks recognise any of them?'

We faced her. There was a dusting of freckles on her cheeks; however it was the look of joy in her blue eyes that convinced me that we were sharing something heavenly. Ryan pointed to a bush near her.

'That's a male Brimstone. The females are green. Apparently, the name butterfly came from the colour of their wings,' he said indicating the graceful pale-yellow creature. 'And ... that one's a Great Purple Hairstreak.'

'What about the green one here?'

'Sorry. I don't know that one, miss. In fact, even though I do recognise most of them, it doesn't matter, does it? Common names ... Latin names. Who cares? Let's just enjoy the show.'

She nodded in understanding as one beautiful Hairstreak alighted on her outstretched arm. We walked on, sharing conversations from time to time with complete strangers or joining in family groups as the children squealed in joy at their immersion in these dancing fields of colour. Quite a few were interested in

118

sharing Ryan's knowledge and we met other amateur butterfly enthusiasts, each enraptured by the swarm around us.

During a lull of conversation where we waited with the wheelchair and hamper, Emma was with some other children a few feet away.

'It's remarkable,' I told Ryan. 'Thank you for bringing us.' Gazing into his dark eyes, it wasn't the time to explain my desire to keep my distance but I would have to do it soon. I owed it to him.

'Amber. There's something I have to tell you.'

I shifted on my feet. Perhaps ...?

'Remember the yellow Brimstone?' he queried.

Suddenly, I felt weak. I moved the hamper and sat down on the chair. I took a deep breath, trying to focus. 'The yellow one?'

'Yes, Amber. Darndest thing. It's not found in the Americas.' That was a shock. This Kaleidoscope was rapidly taking on a more sinister aspect.

'Are you certain, Ryan? I mean ...

you're no expert.' He'd made a mistake. It was the only logical explanation.

Ryan fished into his shoulder bag and drew out his tablet.

'Damn. No internet.' He checked his phone as I did mine. No signal. Very unusual. 'And my watch has stopped,' he added. Then he drew out a book on Lepidoptera identification and showed me the Brimstone. He had been right.

'My watch stopped too. Along with no internet?' I commented while keeping a wary eye on Emma. 'What does it all mean? There's usually no problem with wi-fi here.'

'Electromagnetic interference,' a male voice called out from behind. 'Sorry. Couldn't help but overhear, Amber.'

I lifted myself up by my arms to half-swizzle around. 'Solomon? Is the Prof around?' I introduced him to Ryan. Solomon was a meteorologist too but he was based in Tulsa. We'd met a few times over the years.

'No. Back in Galveston for the time being. Quite upset about that television fiasco.'

'I can imagine. I should have been —' I began.

'No Amber. No one thought that. Certainly not Chuck.' He paused, feeling uncomfortable to mention my health, I guessed. 'I'm taking readings for anything strange. The electromagnetic field is off the chart, everything else is normal. You're not here measuring stuff, I assume.'

'No, Solomon. Just here with my daughter.' I glanced around. We all did.

'Is that her?' my colleague asked, indicating Emma talking with a young woman near a big elm.

'Yes,' I beamed, proudly. He made his excuses at that point, before leaving.

'See you around, Amber. Take care, y'all.'

'You too, Solomon.' He'd obviously been uncomfortable seeing me as I now was. Usually, there'd be a hug and peck on the cheek. Not today, it seemed. Then, as if realising that, he turned his head and grinned.

'I'm off to the game this afternoon. Golden Hurricanes are playing Arkansas State. Should be brilliant.'

'Enjoy yourself, Solomon.' Once he was well out of earshot I asked Ryan if he was into watching sports. He shook his head.

'Thank goodness for that,' I said as I moved the chair around. Emma was talking to the same woman and was leading her back to us.

'Look who I found, Mommy. The weather lady — Maddy.'

'Maddy or Madison. Either is fine with me although the telly people think Maddy's more friendly,' the attractive presenter explained.

I half-stood to shake her hand. Madison was tall, a good two inches taller than me.

'Pleased to meet you. I'm Amber,' I greeted her, introducing Ryan and Emma also. Ryan was nonplussed but graciously polite.

'Pity my daddy's not here, Maddy. He's quite a fan.'

'Yes. He calls you a fluff-bunny,' Emma blurted out before I could stop her. Both Madison and Ryan burst into laughter. I had to join in, too.

Madison knelt to hug Emma. 'Yeah. I guess that's how most viewers would see me; perfect teeth, good looks but without a brain. Those damn skimpy skirts my boss insists I wear, don't help me to be taken seriously much either. Doesn't matter now though. I doubt I'll last the week at the station; Lachlan blinking Peabody will see to that.' She appeared quite sad at the thought.

'Despite what your dad and probably you believe, I am a qualified meteorologist. Duke University and a Masters at Lancaster University in England.' She shrugged. '*The Breakfast Show* pays the bills but it hardly stretches my mind. And then there's the reporting about anything and everything inane. I hate most of it. Today's great but usually ...' She paused, trying to smile. 'My husband ...'

'You're married?'

Madison flashed her ring, her face

brightening. 'Very happily, in fact. Can't wear this on screen. Lachlan says it spoils my wholesome girl-next-door image.' Then she looked at my face. 'I know you too. Amber Devane; author of *The Green Skies Scenario*. It was a brilliant treatise you wrote.' She stared up past the high canopy above us. 'Seems a bit green up there right now. You did predict changes in animal behaviour and these little critters being here certainly fit the bill.'

She continued, her bright eyes and cheerful disposition rubbing off on me. 'My cameraman, Leroy, got some great footage of me with an expert entomologist who's having the time of her life here.' Madison flipped over her notebook. 'Said she's identified some long-extinct butterfly ... here it is; It's Glaucopsyche xerces; the Xerces Blue. She thought that it might have been its cousin, the Silvery Blue, but it isn't.'

Ryan became visibly excited too. 'The Xerces Blue? No way. it's been extinct since 1941. California. There's a photo in here ... ' He opened his book, showing

Emma and us. His face was all lit up like Emma's on Christmas morning.

Madison and I looked at one another.

'Ryan's a — ' I started.

'Nerd? Don't go and say 'nerd', Amber. You of all people,' he interrupted, suddenly angry.

I clasped his hand. 'I was going to say 'an expert'. He's a school friend helping me out after ... a rough patch in my life. He's an astronomer.'

I felt the ire drain from him. The school bullies had affected him far more than I thought. His insecurity was still there under his strong façade.

Ryan cleared his throat. 'Excuse me, ladies. My tummy's rumbling something awful. Do you reckon, you two might like to move on to see the show? We can find a nice vantage point and have our food. Maddy, you're welcome to join us. Seems you weather girls have loads to chat about.'

Madison nodded. 'That would be super, Ryan. I'm supposed to be doing this segment for tonight's local news but

I'm certain Lachlan will veto it. Him and me don't see eye to eye these days, after...' She glanced at Emma who was totally engrossed with the flying insects.

'After he made some unwelcome advances to me. I rejected him. Not a happy cowboy at all.'

We didn't say much as we headed off to the nexus. The butterflies were everywhere. There seemed to be tens of thousands. We gasped. So many rainbow-coloured creatures fluttering around or sitting on plants or the sparse grasses.

'How's about over yonder?' Ryan indicated.

'Perfect,' we agreed.

★ ★ ★

After setting out our picnic on a rug which Ryan had thoughtfully brought, Madison and I arranged the food and drinks while Emma and Ryan explored the scene not far from us. We kept the food covered as the insects were both numerous and inquisitive.

Peering at Emma sometimes, I saw her skipping through the wildflowers. She loved the freedom out here. Our apartment in Galveston had never been my plan for her to grow up in. It had been Joshua who'd said 'No' to any place with a yard.

Whenever she'd seen them in parks, Emma had seemed to have a special affinity for the tiny creatures. More than once, I'd noticed a group of them flocking to her while she'd asked them endless questions about their adventures. Her fairy friends, she'd called them.

Gazing upwards, I gestured all around us to Maddy.

'Look around you at this ... this *miracle*. Excuse me while take a second to see it for what it is — to appreciate the beauty and the joy that all of these other people are here to witness.'

I'd always loved the insects' delicate majesty and today ... well, this was one hell of a butterfly collection.

We studied the scene. Children were playing and laughing while adults watched, themselves captivated by the multi-hued spectacle. A few were sharing their picnics with the insects. Some butterflies flocked to honey-smeared slices of bread while others preferred saucers with rotting fruit, brought especially for the occasion. Young children, teenagers and adults of all ages joined in the experience.

Ryan and Emma came over to us, opening the plastic bottle of honey Emma had brought and tipping some onto a metal lid that Ryan had in his pocket. Immediately two insects alighted to taste it.

It was time for our special picnic. No teddybears, though. Just one gorgeous ambience. Madison and I had an instant connection and it wasn't simply our fascination with the weather.

Once finished, we all lay back on the grass, totally relaxed.

I asked Madison when she needed to go.

'No rush, Amber. Technically I finished my day at noon but Lachan would expect us to work all hours. The station is that jumped-up despot's little fiefdom and we're his serfs. Just because he's conned his way into the boss's good books ... Anyway, I'm not bowing down to him any longer.'

'You could spend the afternoon here with us, if you want, Madison.'

Ryan amazed me. I'd thought he'd want us on our own. I struggled to prop myself up on my elbow to stare at him.

Madison sat up too.

'That would be lovely, if I'm not getting in the way. Glen, my husband, doesn't finish till late and I'd much rather stay here with you guys.'

'Then that's settled,' Emma joined in, once more showing us she wasn't always a little girl. We laughed.

I thought about the weather house in my bedroom and Mr Brolly standing outside. The breeze was already picking up and the warmth of the sunshine gradually dissipating. Maddy, like me, had realised that today would be the last day of good weather for quite some time.

'Thinking about tomorrow, Amber?' she asked.

'Yeah. I just hope we all survive it in one piece.'

5

Life is Not a Fairy Tale

Once upon a time, the weather in Oklahoma was perfect. The sun bathed the fields of crops and cattle during the balmy days while night-time saw the most genteel of showers caressing the lands all around.

Once upon a time.

But life doesn't always have a fairy tale ending. By the time we'd almost reached the family ranch, grey clouds had swallowed the wispy white ones in their frenzied race across the darkened plains and towns.

It was colder too. Ryan had the heater on in his four-by-four. I invited him in although, with one eye on the weather and the knowledge that he had to drive to work tonight, he was reluctant.

Emma had experienced a tiring day, jumping and playing with her fairy friends, and would probably have an early night.

'Ryan. We need to talk. Actually, I'll do the talking. There are some facts you must be informed about, regarding my health. It's why there can't be an 'us', at least till I'm certain.'

His features mirrored his concern as he pulled up into our driveway. 'Okaaay, Amber. I don't really need to go home before work.'

It was only fifteen minutes there and back, but that would have added half an hour to the drive to work in total, as his place was closer to Tulsa.

We had to dash inside as the gusts where tossing dust and anything not nailed down all over. Ryan carried Emma, protecting her eyes from the dirt. Things were becoming unsettled, exactly as I'd thought they would.

'Land a goshen,' Mom declared as we bundled through the back door. She pushed it to, the minute we were in. 'Where did that wind spring up from? It was calm a few minutes ago when I brought in the sheets.'

'Green Skies, Mom. Remember? This is just the beginning. Are Dad and Rusty inside?'

As if by enchantment, they both appeared although my father was definitely worse for wear.

'Daddy. What happened?'

He grinned sheepishly before hobbling over to Gramps Dexter's old rocker. His hand was bandaged and there were grazes on his forearm and cheek.

'Dang tractor bit me, sweetheart. T'ain't nothing. Just a scratch or two.'

Even so, there was a pallor to his skin that wasn't right. His deep blue eyes were sullen as well. I intended to mention it but figured Mom was the nurse and would act if there were anything serious amiss. It was only later that we discovered she had other things on her mind.

Eventually, he explained what had happened. His new pride-and-joy had stopped without reason on the way to the field. Thinking the battery was flat, he began tinkering with it only to receive one almighty jolt of electricity.

'Good thing I had my cell phone in my overalls, 'cause it tossed me ten foot onto my patootie. Hurt like … well, it hurt a lot.'

Emma was listening intently so Dad was trying his best. Mom didn't agree and gave him a withering glare.

'Electric shock? Dad, that can stop your heart,' I blurted out, conscious that a shock had restarted mine but could also be fatal.

'Tush and nonsense, Amber. Your old daddy's as tough as old boots. Take more than that to …' It was then he must have realised the reason for my distress because he immediately changed the subject.

'And how was your day, Miss Emma?' he asked her. 'See any of them margarine flies?'

I'd left a note, explaining where we'd gone.

Emma laughed, despite her lethargy.

'Butterflies, Grandpa. There were millions of them.' She put her arms out to try and convey the number. 'And Ryan bought me a butterfly T-shirt and colouring book and we met Maddy.'

'Whoa! Slow down, little one. You met Maddy?'

I decided to make him squirm a little.

'Madison knows all about fluff-bunnies too, Dad. Emma told her.'

Dad blushed. 'Oh my. I 'spose I'd best watch what I say in future?'

'Sounds like an excellent idea to me, too,' Mom replied. 'Now. Anyone for a nice hot drink? It's gone mighty cold in here all a sudden.'

I checked the outside temperature sensor on the kitchen wall. Thirty-eight? That couldn't be right. It was in the seventies this morning.

'Mom?' I said. 'OK if Ryan joins us for dinner? Seems pointless, him heading home then back in an hour or so for work.'

'Sure. Cornbread, pork, potatoes and squash fine for you, my boy? Pecan pie for dessert?'

'Sounds fine to me, Rhonda. Anything that needs closing up out there? Chickens? Barn?'

Before Mom could answer, I told her I wanted to speak to Ryan in private.

'Go on. You young 'uns can go in the parlour. I'll make a start on our meal and your daddy can look at the presents that Emma's dying to show him. I bet you got some dandy photos too on that fancy phone of yours, Amber. You can show us later. Right now, get going, you two. Skedaddle.'

★ ★ ★

Conversations about your own health concerns are always difficult to have with those close to you. Admittedly we'd only become reacquainted again a few days since, yet in many ways, I felt closer to Ryan than I had to Josh. I wanted to protect him in one way. In another, I felt I was baring my soul. To elaborate about my op was hard enough. It was even worse explaining the all-pervasive feeling of vulnerability I'd had since.

The what-if scenarios were there in my mind. What if I'd died on the operating table, or did so in the uncertain future? I had no doubt Mom and Dad would step up to the years-long task of raising my precious Emma, but they were no spring chickens. Then there was the question of how it would affect Emma, losing both her parents.

I tried to explain all of this to Ryan, tempering my confession with reservations about placing my burden on his shoulders. As I hoped, he listened carefully, offering up his own reassurances that he would be there for me, no matter what.

There was nothing left to say. He enfolded me in his arms and kissed my forehead over and over until my sobbing stopped. At least now he knew.

* * *

The meal was pleasant yet subdued. Ryan had gone outside to make certain all was locked up against the wind. At least the tractors, including the Steiger, were under cover. It had started without a problem when our neighbour responded to dad's distress call after he'd been shocked. He'd brought Dad back home and patched him up. Most ranchers could turn their hands to anything, even basic doctoring.

The winds had abated somewhat, thank goodness. Suspecting that the weather could change without warning, I felt concerned for Ryan driving up to the observatory. It wasn't that far, though it was isolated and up a winding road near Stillwater. He pulled his Parka over his head and zipped it up. I went with him to the door.

'Thanks for today, Ryan. It was extra special for Emma — and for me. You are such a wonderful man. I'm sorry that ...'

I left the sentence unfinished. Sometimes words weren't enough to explain my feelings; attraction yet fear to commit. Damn.

'You take care, Mister. Phone me when you get there. Just to let me know you're all right.'

'Sure, Amber.' He moved his face to kiss me goodbye but, seeing me pull back slightly, decided otherwise.

Although I could understand his reaction, if he had kissed me, I wouldn't have objected. After all, as the song said, *A kiss is just a kiss.*

He was out of the door and running to his vehicle before I could change my mind.

I watched from the window until he'd driven off then returned to my family. It was almost time for the local news. I expected Madison's report would be shown.

'Ryan get off OK, Amber?' Mom asked.

'Yes. And I did try and explain.'

'He's a good man, sweetheart. The best.'

'I realise that, Mom. That's what

makes it so aggravating.'

It was dusking outside as we settled down facing the new-ish smart screen telly I'd bought for my parents last Christmas.

There were reports on the State Fair and Tulsa's sporting heroine of the moment, some tennis player. Just before the end, a pre-recorded report from Madison, at the Kaleidoscope, came on. Emma was elated to see her new friend and to see the nexus again in full-flight.

The interview with the expert and photos of the not-so-extinct Xerces Blue butterfly were shown, yet it was disappointingly obvious that all of Maddy's speculation about the causes and the Green Skies was edited out. It was a report simply about an unusual happening. I suspected Lachlan had sabotaged her much more interesting account. She came across once again as a pretty but vapid reporter rather than the talented, incisive scientist that she was.

Dad was strangely quiet. Was he feeling guilty for his old-fashioned sexist attitude to her?

We'd permitted Emma to stay up simply because of the programme. She was yawning by the time it had finished.

'Beddy-bye time, my precious,' I told her. She was already in her Barbie nightwear and had brushed her teeth.

As we said good night and walked to the hall, Emma gasped, 'Mommy, look. It's white rain.'

I followed her gaze. Snow? In May?

She'd never seen it for real.

Mom and Dad joined us at the window. It was quite heavy and gusting, coming in almost horizontally at times. It was sticking too, giving the yard a surreal dusting of white. The outside temperature was twenty-eight, well below freezing. Then there was the wind chill, which would make it seem much colder. We were lucky that the LPG heating was switched on.

Of course, it took a bit longer to convince a very enthralled young lady to get to bed. I was pretty darn certain it would be there for her in the morning, all lovely and fleecy and ready for snowman building. In the end, there was a sort of compromise — she could lie in bed and watch the snowfall through the window as I would leave the drapes open.

She snuggled up to her teddy and her other furry friends in bed. I'd brought all of our personal stuff from Galveston in a removal van once I and Joshua had parted ways. Emma had settled into her new bedroom right away once we'd brought her childhood treasures in. As I closed the door, her tiny voice was relating the day's adventures to her unspeaking companions.

I'd hardly sat down again when we heard the back doorbell.

'Who can that be?' Dad wondered. 'It's a blizzard out there.'

'Maybe Bigfoot come a-calling?' Mom suggested.

'We won't find out unless someone answers,' I replied, struggling to my feet. It rang again before I could answer it. The deadlock and bolts were on so I had to find the keys.

At last the door opened. Without being asked, a snow-clad figure pushed past me into the room.

'About time, Amber. A fella could freeze to death out there.'

It was Ryan. He threw his hood back, scattering flakes of snow all over the cedarwood floor. Without ceremony he hung up his wet jacket and pulled off his boots, leaning on the door frame to do so. I grabbed a towel and passed it to him.

'How come you're back here, my boy?' Dad asked from his armchair. 'Get yerself lost?'

'No, Barry. My co-worker phoned and told me not to bother with work. He was snowed in and, with all the clouds, not much we could do there tonight. Good thing too. The roads are really bad news. I decided to turn around and return here. That snow's drifting. Even with my four-wheel drive, I got stuck coming back. Had to hoof it the last half mile.'

'You want to bunk down here, Ryan? No problem. Have to be the couch though,' Mom told him. 'Hopefully it'll ease off tomorrow.' She went to brew up some hot coffee for him.

'Thanks, Rhonda. My hands are frozen. Who'd have thought I'd need gloves this late in spring? I hate snow. It's only suitable for postcards in my opinion. Though I figure young Emma will love it.'

Mom then shocked me by suggesting I do something to 'warm the poor man up'.

'Mom!' I protested. Blood rushed to my face.

Everyone turned to me.

'Gracious, Amber. I didn't mean anything like that, 'specially not in front of your daddy and me. Get him one of your father's sweaters. Can't you see him shivering?'

Ryan grinned at my discomfort. What had I been thinking? Making a fool of yourself once more, Amber Devane. Whenever will you learn?

After bringing out an old, clean sweater and helping Mom find blankets,

I decided to excuse myself. Emma hadn't been the only one to have an exhausting day.

I took my medication and, on reflection, a pain killer that I'd also been given at the hospital. Mom would change my dressings tomorrow. I doubted any nurse would be driving out to do a home visit for a while. This snow would be staying around.

'Goodnight all,' I said, yawning behind my hand.

Daddy was looking sleepy himself even though it was early. He perked up when I stood to leave.

'What, no kiss?' he asked. Although it was usual, with Ryan there I felt self-conscious.

I did the rounds, giggling a little when I reached my astronomer friend. His lips were puckered up ready for mine.

'In your dreams, spaceman,' I told him. 'Cheek only.' He pouted and rubbed his eyes as if crying yet accepted my goodnight kiss without any fuss.

'Before you ask, Ryan Crayson, no,

you can't tuck me in.'

I left them with a spring in my step at the friendly repartee. It had been a good day. Moreover, I'd not felt the need to nod off during the afternoon even though I certainly needed any beauty sleep that I could manage.

★ ★ ★

I awoke at two forty-three. That is, according to my old red-lit LED alarm clock. I'd left the drapes open to enjoy the view but there was none. The entire glass was a sheet of minute white flakes. The wind outside sounded like a wild animal enraged and hungry for blood.

My mouth was as dry as the Nevada desert but I must have forgotten to bring in a glass. This time I could swing out of bed easier. Then, making sure I had both feet on the carpet like I'd been told by the physio at the hospital, I pushed myself up. The room was still warm so I didn't bother with my housecoat, just the slippers. Big mistake.

I was into the living room before I realised the light was on. Ryan looked up at me from the couch where he was under a blanket, reading. I'd forgotten he was here.

'Très chic,' he commented, admiring my attire. It was the dowdiest of nightwear, a well-worn white linen number with giant dots of faded red to complete the picture. I declare. I looked like a walking case of poison ivy rash.

'Did you want anything, Amber?' he said before I could apologise and retreat to my hideyhole. 'Coffee? tea? … Me?'

It was a parody of some old movie or book about a stewardess. He was wearing his glasses, wire-rimmed rather than the dreadful thick black-rimmed ones he'd worn at school. I guessed he'd taken his contacts out.

'Hardly you, Mr Crayson. Some cranberry juice, if you must know.'

I didn't bother lowering my voice too much as the other bedrooms were well away. The snow somehow deadened sound inside too.

I tipped my head to the side and pushed my bangs back from my forehead. There was no point trying to disguise my tatty appearance from him. Any illusions of my sophisticated beauty that he might have harboured were shattered.

'Anyways. What are you doing awake? Couch too lumpy?'

'You forget, my spotted angel. I'm usually awake at night. Body clock is upside down. Just going over some figures from the past few weeks and getting my thoughts together. I'm due to lecture at the university on Tuesday. Some astrophysics symposium.'

I was impressed, though I tried not to show it.

'Once a nerd, always a nerd. With my good looks and your brains ...' I left the sentence hanging. I must have been half-asleep to have been thinking about children.

It was yet another awkward silence.

'Grab your drink, and one for me too, please. And then you can join me on my couch. I'll even let you share my blanket

148

if you're cold.'

Deciding not to respond, I did as he'd asked, though declining the blanket. We sat next to one another for a moment, listening to the blizzard vent its fury while we were safe inside. It was a bizarre situation.

'Thanks for staying, Amber. Given what you were saying earlier, I expected that sitting here by my side would be the last thing you'd want to do.'

'Far from it, my friend. I've shared so much with you in these past few days about me ... about us. We have a connection far deeper than the one I had with Joshua. If 'un I were in the mood for love ...' I took his hand and squeezed it. 'But I'm not and at least you understand why. My head spins so fast at times, I figure I'm caught in the grand-daddy of all twisters. Then I've found you, reaching up to try and give me hope and stability.

'You're my anchor, Ryan. Despite everything I am and all that I'm doing to you right now, you're not turning your back on me or running away. That means so much.'

His dark eyes met mine as he answered. 'I was your friend at college. Back then we were both raw and exposed. We both understand the person inside. As we all grow older, we learn to accept who we are inside but mostly shroud it in some protective shell to disguise the real us. You and me. We don't need that when we're together.

'I can see that you're shattered, in a way,' he continued. 'You've lost that brash confidence you had when you were 'Killer', ready to rescue victims like me and Carla. You were like the Lone Ranger riding to save us. All I could do was try to be your faithful 'Indian' friend, Tonto, riding by your side.'

It hurt to hear it, yet he was so right.

'You said 'Indian' rather than 'native American', Ryan. Sarcasm?'

'Not really. To my grandfather's and father's generations that's what we were to the so-called white men, certainly in movies and telly. It's so stupid really. I mean, the great Christopher Columbus thought America was India so my ancestors were called Red Indians for centuries. Doesn't say much for your ancestors, does it, angel?'

Then he grinned.

He'd been having me on. Typical Ryan.

'I never thought of you as Cherokee, mixed-race or any other group. You were my friend. Being labelled in a box is so wrong. I realise all those 'dumb blonde' jokes I got were nothing compared to what you put up with. You've never really talked about your family.'

'Not much to say. Mom was white, Dad was Cherokee. I ended up being part of neither world so I chose my own life and I'm content with that. People are more tolerant these days. When Mom passed, Dad took to drinking, reinforcing the old stereotype. Funny thing is, loads of the name-callers are drunks too but it's OK for them —' He paused, a little pent-up rage seeping through.

'Do you know much of the Cherokee part of your life?'

Ryan smiled. 'Yeah — a lot, actually.

My grandfather follows the old ways. Still lives in his own ti-pi, sort of, and he taught me the heritage and language. All my Dad's generation had as a role model was Indians shooting white women and children on the telly. You can only hear the words *dirty filthy injun* so many times before you feel ashamed of who you really are. *Dances With Wolves* helped change that, but it was too late for him.'

It was lovely listening to Ryan talk about his life. Mine was an open book to him. I took a sip of juice.

'I would love to meet your grandfather, Ryan. I assume he speaks English?'

'Oh yeah, especially the swear words. He's got them down to a fine art. Speaks Spanish too, at least well enough to get by. He's a member of the Cherokee Nation tribe and, although he's a hermit, he's still well-respected. He taught me a lot over the years, despite Dad's indifference.'

I stood and padded over to a window that wasn't covered by snowflakes. Turning on a light outside showed how fierce yet mesmerising the snow flurries were. There was a good foot on the ground, more where it had drifted.

Ryan joined me.

'Could you tell me what the Cherokee would believe about this bizarre weather?' I asked.

'Well. There's the Great Spirit, Unetlanvhi. He created everything, although I'm not sure if we should say 'he' …

'The way I figure it, this weather would be down to the Great Thunder and his mischievous sons, the Thunder Boys. They wear rainbows and lightning, anything to do with the skies. The priests tried to placate them and ask them for the rain to grow the crops like corn. There's a Green Corn Ceremony. Grandfather has taken me to a few. I should have felt connected but I didn't. I felt proud and humbled but, as I said, I have to walk my own trail.'

We chatted for a while longer until I excused myself for bed again, Ryan promised that he'd grab a few hours too. He would be on leave for the next few nights so there wasn't pressure to get to the observatory, even if the blizzard diminished. That was one consolation, at least.

We had no idea how long this storm would last so I was eager to find out the latest from the weather centre. Tomorrow, I resolved that I'd log on to my NWS account and discover what the Thunder Boys were really doing up there.

★ ★ ★

Upon waking, I chose to spend a half-hour on my laptop. The weather hadn't changed, although at least I could witness the extent of the covering as the windows were clear in places. I couldn't believe we'd been at the warm Kaleidoscope less than a day earlier. The wi-fi kept dropping out, an indication that electronics and any sort of electromagnetism was being ravaged from up above. My watch was still stopped and we'd had no cell phone signals for at least a day. Ryan had been lucky to get a message from the observatory so signals were seemingly there yet sporadic.

Logging on to my sites, I could ascertain that the precipitation wasn't going to alter. All around Tulsa the satellite feed showed a solid blob for over eighty miles in all directions. Outside of that, the rest of Okie and the other states were experiencing warm, sunny weather. I watched a time progression over the past day. Elsewhere, the weather marched west to east as usual; everywhere apart from our patch of country. The Green Sky pattern had grabbed hold of T-Town and environs and was hanging onto it for dear life.

There was no rush to get up as it was obvious no one was budging from my folks' ranch-house for quite awhiles. The thought of Ryan being stuck here too wasn't a problem for me. In fact, I enjoyed his company, being my age and all. Mom fussed too much, Dad was, well ... Dad and love her though I did, conversations with Emma weren't that stimulating.

I showered and made my way to breakfast.

'Morning, sleepyhead. Sleep well?' Mom gave me a gentle squeeze as did my little girl. She'd already eaten and went back to her jigsaw eagerly, happy to amuse herself rather than expecting an adult to play with her. I noticed Ryan, giving her a helpful suggestion about a difficult piece now and then.

That left me and Mom free to catch up. Ryan was watching the breakfast show with interest.

'Where's Dad? Not like him to sleep in. Not that there's much he could do, looking at the state of things out there.'

'Said he didn't feel right well. Might be that battery zap yesterday. I'll take him some coffee in a tick,' my mother answered.

I sat down to my meal. Mom would check my operation cuts later and change the bandages.

I ate in silence listening to the telly for any reports about the events. Strangely, it was mostly federal and overseas reports, plus interviews with 'famous' people no one had ever heard of. Mom was quite content in her own world, making blueberry muffins for later.

I'd finished and was tidying up when I called over to Ryan. 'What's the verdict on this storm? Has Madison mentioned anything?'

He turned his head, his face indicating that he was puzzled. 'Well, she did. Said it wasn't looking good at all. Blizzards changing to torrential rains if the temperature goes up. Even mentioned your Green Skies causing this and warning us to be prepared for the worst. Trouble was, that was over an hour ago. Not seen hide nor hair of her since. Some officious-looking fella's been doing the weather since.'

My attention was drawn to the screen. Going over to the lounge in the open-plan house, I plopped myself next to Emma. Ryan was on the other side of her.

She snuggled up to me, a jigsaw piece in her hand, silently asking for a bit of help. As I made a suggestion, Ryan sat forward.

'That's him. The replacement weatherman.'

I sat forward too. 'It can't be. That's Lachlan Peabody. He knows as much about weather as Emma understands nuclear physics; probably less.' Emma stopped to regard me, on hearing her name. I ruffled her hair.

'He's not the low-life that gave your boss such a hard time the other night, is he, Amber?' Ryan clearly had firm opinions, ready to stand up for my friends.

'Yep. The one and only. What's he saying about the forecast?' I pressed rewind and turned the sound up. Mom joined us, leaning over the back of the settee to watch.

Lachlan wore a suit, not the usual attire for a casual breakfast show. His bright orange cravat was poorly tied but was so obviously an indication of his pretentiousness. As for the man himself, his was not a face that I could take to. Tight mousy brown curls coming to a widow's peak and a moustache straight out of the Seventies. Moreover, he had the sort of roundish baby-face that wasn't quite right, giving him a sinister, untrustworthy air. Even his high-pitched voice caused me to shiver.

'We've had an updated forecast, y'all. Today's snow flurries will be gone in no time leaving us with some wonderful sunshine again. The bit of rain and snow we've had have freshened our gorgeous Oklahoma fields and forests and I can assure you summer is definitely on its way here. I'll leave you good folks with this satellite photo. Y'all have a great day now and I'll see you on my Lachlan Peabody Talk Show at six-thirty where we'll have a special encore performance from Tibbles the singing cat. This is your favourite ol' best friend saying, be good — an' if'un y'all can't be good, be careful.'

Then he gave a sleazy wink. We were totally dumbfounded. I wished I'd not had that bacon.

'Rewind to the sat photo, Amber, then

pause it,' Ryan said after recovering. 'There's something that caught my eye.'

I did as he asked, pressing *pause* when he said. 'Top left, Amber. The date.'

Although I'd missed it the first time around, the date of the benign weather image was from two weeks earlier. He'd deliberately falsified the forecast, shattering the trust between the viewers and the integrity of the United States National Weather Service.

And when Lachlan's promises of wonderful weather failed to materialise, he'd apologise sincerely and blame my department for passing on erroneous information. It would be our fault and Mister Butter-wouldn't-melt would shrug his slightly too broad shoulders and grin.

'He's taken over Maddy's spot and is lying through his teeth to T-Town, Amber. But why?' Ryan was the angriest I'd ever seen him, even at college. His knuckles were white as he clenched and unclenched his smooth hands.

'No idea, my friend,' I replied. 'There's

another question that needs answering, though. What has he done with Madison?'

6

Family Problems

I didn't hesitate. Whether it was the anger or something else, the dull pain that was there in my body was pushed aside as I stood to retrieve my cell phone from the bedroom.

As expected, there was no signal. Madison and I had exchanged phone numbers yesterday. Dear Lord. Was it only yesterday? The warmth of the Kaleidoscope and lying on the grass together seemed like a world away. Outside the winds blew and the snow continued to swirl past my window.

I'd met people like Lachlan before in my career; luckily, not too many times. They had some sort of misplaced god complex, believing that they should be the centre of attention. Maybe such individuals didn't understand that simply because they believed they were there to be in charge, did not mean that they deserved to be. Often, they had no qualities or talents to offer, other than the questionable ability to manipulate others for their own selfish reasons.

I hadn't actually met Mr Peabody — but, from everything I'd seen, he wasn't a trustworthy man.

Returning, I picked up the landline phone to try Maddy's cell. Nothing again. It was a fair bet the Green Skies above the snow clouds were screwing up all sorts of communication links. Checking my handbag again, I retrieved her home number. She'd told me that she and her husband owned a house in the suburbs of T-Town, not far from the television studio.

I tried it and was pleased to hear it ringing out.

'Hello,' a female voice answered. It didn't sound like my new friend.

'Is that you, Maddy?'

'No. It's her mother-in-law, Peggy Sue. Who's this?'

'Amber Devane. Madison and I met yesterday.'

'Ah, yes. Madison mentioned you, Amber. She's pretty darn upset. I came over when I heard what happened at the station. I don't think she's up to talking … ' I heard another voice in the background asking who it was. Peggy Sue said my name and the voice said to pass her the phone.

'Are you sure?' Peggy Sue asked before relinquishing the handset.

'Hi Amber, Just a sec.' I heard her reassuring Peggy Sue that it would be OK before getting back on the line to me.

When she returned, I expressed concern, saying that we'd just watched Lachlan taking over her spot on the weather bulletin, and making a right pig's ear of it, too.

'He was lying, Maddy. Out and out blatant lies.'

When she replied, I could sense the hurt and anger in her sweet voice.

'It's what he does, Amber. He's a … I

164

don't recall what the word is for someone without a conscience.'

'Politician?' I suggested. Madison laughed, saying she needed that release. Then I told her the real name. 'Sociopath.'

'Yeah … That's him, all right. He sacked me on the spot for not following his maniacal instructions about burying the terrible weather in store for us.'

I was shocked. 'Lachlan sacked you? Can he even do that? He's just a jumped-up anchorman.'

'He was. He's in charge now that Shirley is on leave. They became lovers soon after he came to the station and he's been worming his way up the pecking order ever since. Now he's determined to quash anyone that doesn't agree with him and his irrational beliefs.'

'Oh,' was all I could say. Office politics, gone mad. The trouble was that T-Town was not only in difficulty meteorologically — but also the channel to warn and advise them was being hijacked.

'Surely your proper boss wouldn't

agree to your dismissal like that? What has she told you when you let her know, Maddy?'

There was a pause.

'I haven't contacted her. I can't. Shirl went off the normal radar following some sort of family emergency. Said she needed to focus on the situation. Originally, she left Trevor McShane in charge though she must have changed her mind. Lachlan circulated a copy e-mail she sent to him, asking that he take over. Trevor tried to ring but all her contact numbers are either unobtainable or disconnected.'

It was a nightmare. Huge numbers of communication networks were so much junk at the present time. I quizzed Madison further on any other way to catch up with Shirley. She explained that she'd tried everything.

Realising that it was down to me to intervene, I told Madison to keep trying and that I'd ring her later. I had other phone calls to make urgently.

★ ★ ★

Placing the phone on its charger, I filled in Mom and Ryan on events. Like me, they weren't happy.

'What are you planning on doing, darling?' Mom said to me. 'We don't want you getting too involved just yet. You're not well.'

Emma had wandered off, bored with the adult conversation. She'd finished the jigsaw and was no doubt searching for something to do. As I looked around the room, I saw her and Rusty standing by the window. They both wanted to go outside.

She came over. She had that endearing pleading look in her wide grey eyes.

'Mommy. The white rain has stopped. Can me and Rusty go outside now?'

She was right. It was still gusting although not as bad.

'In a little while, my lovely. Mommy has some important phone calls to make.'

The disappointment clouded her cherubic features and, for a few seconds, I hated myself. Emma returned to the window, saying nothing.

'I could take her,' Ryan suggested, quietly. 'Those hens need tending to in any case. Seems like Barry's taking the day off.'

He was trying to help and once again I could sense the caring, goodness inside him.

'That would be great, Ry — ' I began.

'No!' my mom said firmly but still in a whisper so as not to upset Emma.

'I beg your pardon?' was my angry reaction.

'Don't take that tone with me, Amber Louise.' My mom was still seated in between Ryan and me but had pulled back angrily. 'Those 'important' calls of yours can wait. Your Emma is seeing snow for the first time in her young life and she wishes to go outside to play in it. And she'd love to share that experience with her mommy … you.

'And you'll want that memory. Photos and video can only do so much. You can take Ryan, too, for the strenuous stuff. Can't have you messing up those stitches when we can't get you back to the hospital. Well, I said my piece. Up to you, girl. Just remember, I was there with you when you first played in the snow. Or had you forgotten?'

I was shocked at her outburst, especially with Ryan watching. Emma hadn't budged so hopefully, she'd not heard the fight. Actually, not so much a fight as a well-deserved telling-off. I wasn't too irritated to understand that she was one hundred per cent right.

I grinned. 'Yes, Mom. I remember that first snow fight. We ganged up on Dad if I recall. When did you become so bossy, though? You've never interfered between Emma and me before.'

She smiled back, giving me a peck on the cheek. 'Never needed to. You are a great mom. As for being bossy, I've always been like that inside. Just choose my battles. Ask your daddy. Speaking of Barry, where is that man? Not like him to be a sleeping in like a groundhog in winter.'

I leaned over the settee back to call to my little girl. The weather was currently calm.

'Emma, sweetheart. Grab your warmest clothes and gloves. Guess where you, me and Ryan are going?'

Her little face was suddenly transformed.

'Outside into the snow.'

'You bet your booties, Emma,' said Ryan, lifting her up. 'And you and I and your mommy are gonna build a snowman.'

'Wowee.'

'I'll fetch the old video camera to catch the action, although my snowball fights are well and truly done. Come on, everybody. You too, Rusty.'

★ ★ ★

It took me much longer than Emma to get ready. She was dressed in her Parka, rain boots, gloves and woolly hat and scarf whereas I was struggling with my coat. My side was paining. I tried not to wince. Ryan stepped in to assist.

When we stepped outside, the white flakes were falling gently all around, pirouetting as they wafted to the thick, white carpet beneath. Mom was right. I would have regretted missing this moment with Emma for the rest of my life.

At first, my darling daughter paused, trying to take it all in. Her cheeks were rosy in the brisk coolness. It was twenty-eight degrees and her breath formed a little cloud before her face.

Gingerly, she reached out to poke it, then caught a snowflake in her gloved hand, sniffing and watching as it melted before her eyes. She glanced up to me, puzzled.

'Where's it gone, Mommy?'

I explained in simple terms about melting. I think she understood. Behind us, my mom was busy with the camera. Ryan was already gathering snow into a ball. I laughed as he overbalanced and tumbled into the snow. Only his feet, waving frantically, were visible as he struggled.

'We don't need to make a snowman,' I

said to Emma. 'We have a real one right there.'

Ryan was white all over, appearing quite embarrassed. Then he did a silly little dance.

'Shall we join him, my precious?' I asked.

Emma agreed, then noticed Rusty bounding up and down. The layer of white was almost as high as he was.

'Will you hold my hand?' Emma asked. It was a moment of wanting to explore this wintery wonderland yet being that little bit trepidatious at stepping into the unknown.

'Always,' I told her as we stepped out into the fluffy thickness together. For the following twenty minutes, she gambolled in the snow with me watching and taking a vicarious pleasure in her giggles and delight. Finally, she went off with Ryan to the chicken enclosure to feed them and collect the eggs, assuming they were laying.

I returned inside, realising that the bracing cold had tired me. Although

Mom had come back in earlier, she was nowhere to be seen. Taking off my damp outer clothes to hang them up, I called out if she wanted a hot drink. There was no answer so I switched on the coffee maker, choosing a caramel macchiato pod from the box in the cupboard.

I drank it quickly, feeling my numb insides gradually thawing. Holding the warm cup in both hands helped too.

It was only as I was savouring the last mouthful that Mom appeared from the hallway. Her drawn expression told me that something was wrong.

Before I could ask, Ryan and Emma entered through the back door.

'It's Barry. He's really ill. I've just found him on the floor and put him back in bed. His temperature is over one hundred.'

'Infection?' Ryan was there in an instant after shucking off all his wet gear and pants protectors.

'Yeah. Cut himself the other day in the barn. Silly old galoot didn't think nothing of it till later. He put some disinfectant on it. Seems like he waited too long. He's feverish and can't think straight. Weak as a kitten too.'

'Tetanus?' I asked.

'Oh, his shots for lockjaw are up to date. This is a different bacterial bug and I've done as much as I can do with what we's got here.

'What he really needs is an antibiotic. A broad-spectrum one. Trouble is we're stuck out here.'

We all turned to the window. The blizzard was back in all its fury, the winds screaming a warning to all not to venture out.

Ryan was standing, helplessly. I hated to ask the next question, but we had to hear.

'How long has he got, Mom?'

She fought back tears.

'Not much time at all. Hours at the most.'

7

The Road to Hell

We discussed the few options available. Medical help coming to us was a very slim possibility. Mom could ring her hospital though, without antibiotics, there was little they could suggest that she wasn't already doing.

The outside temperature display caught my attention. It was climbing. Opening my laptop, I accessed our Tulsa weather centre. Indications were that there was a continuing temperature increase forecast around us, which would steadily turn the blizzard of snow to sleet and maybe rain.

I told everyone what I'd hoped. Once we had rain, the snow would melt quickly, much faster than if there were no rain.

Outside it read thirty degrees — still below freezing. Upper atmosphere readings on my website showed a parallel gradient up there where the snow was forming.

'Mom. Is Daddy fit to travel?'

'He'll have to be. What are you thinking?'

'Our car's no good and the tractor's not suitable for transporting him. Therefore, it has to be Ryan's Jeep. But that's stuck in a snowdrift back up the road.'

'The tractor. The new one. That could pull my four by four free,' Ryan suggested. 'Trouble is … I don't have the foggiest how to drive one.'

One step forward, two steps back. It was Mom who reckoned it out, although I sensed that a part of her hesitated to suggest it.

'Listen, everyone. We can't drive to Tulsa in our car, not in the snow or even when it starts to melt. There'll be black ice everywhere. What we need to do is get the four-wheel drive here, ready to take Barry as soon as the snow begins to wash away.' She placed her hands on my shoulders.

'Amber. I want you to go to the

tractor with Ryan. You've driven your share of tractors over the years. Ryan drives, you tell him what to do. You'll enjoy doing that, my girl.' She smirked. 'Retrieve Ryan's Jeep and tow it here, ready for the big melt.' She turned towards where Dad lay in pain in their bed. 'Time is short, so we all have to be ready to go in the Jeep the minute the snow stops. Think you can cope with that, Amber?'

'I'll do all the lifting and driving,' Ryan offered. 'All you'll have to do is look pretty and give me instructions. There are two seats in the tractor, aren't there? Think of it as a fun day out.'

Trust him to try and gee me up.

Ryan was game and so was I. There was nothing more to do but get everyone ready to move at the first sign of a thaw.

We'd all have to go to the hospital. Ryan phoned Mom's workplace in order to put them in the picture as he dressed in his waterproofs. The hospital needed to be ready for my father's arrival. Mom went to start on getting him ready to travel.

That left me to say my goodbyes to Emma, as I put my own waterproofs on. Thinking ahead, I brewed us two Thermoses full of hot, sweet tea and grabbed some muffins. It would be freezing out there and Ryan wasn't a strong man.

There was already a tow-rope in his vehicle. I suggested a towing bar to provide more stability as we'd have to drive the Jeep to the ranch carefully. I simply couldn't hold the Jeep steering wheel to guide it while it was being pulled.

'Emma, darling. Mommy will be going outside for a while. When we return, we have to take Grandpa to the hospital. He's very sick. You'll need to come along and it will be very scary… for all of us. But I need you to be brave and do everything Granny and I tell you. Can you do that, sweetheart?'

I could see the worry in her pretty face but she nodded. I told her to get dressed in her outdoor clothes. Mom would help her.

I knelt to embrace her, whispering words of reassurance. The weather, her grandad being ill, being prepared for a risky journey – it was a lot to expect my four-year-old to take in. She'd already had so much upheaval in her short life.

Ryan knelt too and told her he'd protect me. The look on her face showed that had helped.

* * *

Outside, the gales caught my breath. The wind chill meant it felt much colder than it was. Ryan and I had scarves wrapped around our faces and snow goggles on. Mom had found them in a cupboard in the hall. Ten feet from the house and I was freezing already, despite the thick insulation.

Unable to make myself heard over the shriek of the gales, all I could do was point towards the machinery sheds across the big back yard. Ryan trudged off, then he returned to assist me. Damn. I felt so weak and useless.

By now there was simply whiteness in the air and on the ground. It was so disorienting. For one terrifying moment, I thought we'd gotten lost, heading back on ourselves. There was a yellowish glow ahead. I recalled that Mom had switched on the floodlights outside the shed.

What had been an easy walk yesterday was now like an Arctic trek. Objects scattered on the ground were hidden under two feet of snow, making every step treacherous.

The light drew closer. Finally, we were inside the shelter of the shed. The big doors were open but in the lee of the wind, so there was very little whiteness inside the cavernous structure. It was cold, but dry. Ryan unwrapped his scarf and removed his gloves to fish the key to the Steiger from his jacket pocket. He had a flashlight too.

'Just hope that battery problem Barry had yesterday was a one-off,' he muttered, clambering up into the enclosed cabin.

'It was probably a Green Skies pulse.

The electro-magnetism problems seem to fluctuate.'

I watched from the front, praying that the engine would kick over. It didn't. Dead as the proverbial dodo, despite numerous tries.

Desperately, I examined the other machinery. What else could we employ? Away from the open doors, it was gloomy and hard to see. It had been years since I'd been out here and although every noise reverberated in the vastness, there was a wonderful sense of belonging. The farm meant so much to me. Pity I'd only realised it this late.

My eyes adjusted to the shadows. There it was; Dad's old red Massey, relegated to the corner at the far end. Its battery was probably flat too — but we had no choice but to try it.

Dad kept its key nearby in a tiny workshop at the back. Beginning to run over to retrieve it, I stopped, panting, after three steps.

'I'll get it,' my knight in heavy clothing told me, as if he could sense my intentions. I explained where the keys were. By the time I made my way down to the far end of our massive shed, he was already in the cab. The engine sputtered to life and lights cut through the darkness. I shielded my eyes until they adjusted, moving out of the glare.

'Come on, Amber. Get in,' he called out over the noisy spluttering of the idling engine.

I was out of breath and choking on the fumes. His priority was time to save Dad. That was mine too — in principle. The difficulty was that my body was less enthusiastic. I attempted to climb up but it put a strain on the muscles under my armpit.

Seeing my discomfort, Ryan climbed down and helped me into the cab, gallantly closing the door before resuming his place on the less than comfy driver's seat.

'Thanks,' I gasped, checking out the panel on the dash. He jumped down again, returning with the fixed tow-bar. I'd forgotten we needed that. Talking him through the controls was easy. He checked some points, before switching on even more big lights up on the cabin roof.

'You ready?' I asked him.

'As I'll ever be,' was his response. He shifted it into gear and I turned the air-con heater up high. We needed to be warm.

★ ★ ★

It was a slow journey through the drifts on the road, even though the snow blowing all around us was now wetter. The thermometer outside said thirty-two; freezing point. Not long now, I hoped; soon the snow would melt and be washed away.

Crossing Fink's Ghost Creek, I peered out over the stone walls to the rapids below. The stream wasn't frozen. Instead, its rage reflected the murderous cold within the churning waters. Today, that place where I'd bathed as a child was part of another, more violent world.

We almost missed the Jeep as it was covered with snow. This was going to be harder than I thought, I realised, as Ryan warily turned the big beast around and backed up to where his vehicle was. Cleaning it off was a two-person job. We made sure that the tractor engine kept running.

Once more, I had to stop, gasping from the hard work. My chest burned from inside.

Ryan continued, gratefully accepting the hot drink and nourishment in between working on his Jeep. I could only stand and watch. I felt so useless, although it was evident I'd already pushed myself too far.

Once he'd finished sweeping the wet snow from his vehicle, he attached the tractor using the towing hitch and we set off. As we neared the bridge, I realised I must have dozed off in the heat of the cab.

'Watch out, Ryan,' I yelled in panic. 'The verge!'

He was far too close to the soft edges.

Driving a tractor was so different from a car — especially judging distance.

Too late. We lurched to the side, the narrower front right wheel sinking into the grassy mud. Ryan tried to correct it but the wheel started sliding down the river bank, pulling the front with it. We both fell forward, bracing ourselves. By the time the tractor slithered to a halt, we were three feet below the roadside and staring aghast at the churning white water.

I looked around with difficulty. The Jeep was still on the road but if we slipped any further …

'Sorry, Amber.'

'Quick. I'll detach the tow connector. You jam some rocks under the wheels. And for heaven's sake, man. Be careful.'

Opening my door, I eased myself down onto the slippery grass but, with the sleet and my weakness, my fingers slid off the wet outside. I found myself tumbling down the slope to the water's edge. The frigid waters soaked through to my skin in an instant. I couldn't breathe.

The lower half of my body was under-water, with more splashing over me as it cascaded over the smooth rocks. In an instant I was freezing, my teeth chatter-ing as I shivered, uncontrollably.

A scream was impossible as any sounds were caught in my throat.

Where the hell was Ryan? I peered through half-closed eyes. I was horri-fied at what was there; the front end of the tractor three feet above me and five feet away. I was directly in its path. Even above the deafening river, I heard move-ment as the handbrake creaked again.

I swore loudly. It didn't help. Then I saw Ryan shoving rocks and boulders under all the wheels in a frantic attempt to stabilise the monster ready to crush me. I strained to roll out of the way. He was shrieking at me to move.

Despite my life depending on it, I couldn't. Some branch or debris had pierced my coat and jumper, holding me in its terrifying embrace.

I dreaded hearing the death-knell of the tractor budging again, closing my eyes as I pulled and pulled at whatever had its icy grip on me.

'I'm sorry, Emma,' I sobbed as I struggled with my sleeve, but with the cold and the fear ... Just then I felt something hit my face from up the slope. The tractor must be moving.

8

Then Came the Rains

A hand touched my face. It was Ryan's. 'Stop mumbling and concentrate. Roll over.'

'I ... can't. Arm's stuck.' I wiggled my fingers a little. The cold water was numbing everything including my brain.

Opening my eyes, I watched as he extricated the wood from my sweater and coat. It was an exposed tree root, now scarlet with my blood. Ryan pulled me from the water up the slope. I winced, my side stitches taking a pounding as he dragged me over the rocky bank. The redness on the stick was washing into the water, I noticed.

'Can you stand, Amber? You're a dead weight. I'm so sorry. I almost killed you.'

'Not safe yet, mister. You still might succeed,' I slurred vindictively. Whether in anger or pain, I was lashing out. They were words I'd regret, said in the freezing cold of the moment.

He stopped, seemingly shocked at my violent outburst. The trouble was, he took it to heart. The facts were that he'd saved me when I couldn't save myself. Damn it. That root was so flimsy and yet I'd given up so easily.

He helped me to struggle to my feet, supporting me from the front. All of that time, our faces were inches apart though his eyes were staring at everything else, apart from mine. I was trying to draw strength from him, but his guilt was shutting me out.

'Sorry, Ryan. Shouldn't've blamed you. Accident.'

He didn't respond; simply dropped his gaze to my feet. Once I was balanced, he let go as if afraid to touch me. It was the last thing I wanted.

'You're cold and you're wet. We have to get up to my Jeep and get that started. There's a pathway over here.'

I was shivering as I struggled up the slope on all fours, Ryan behind me. The tow was still attached to the tractor so Ryan quickly unhitched it from the Jeep, leaving me to get inside. He started the engine first go and set the heating to full. There was a blanket on the back seat. He gave it to me, though it was obvious that he was reluctant to touch me or tuck it in.

Within moments, we'd set off. The snow was thawing as the gusting rain pelted down all around us. The blower was warming me and although I could feel my skin temperature increasing, the chill in the air between Ryan and me persisted all the way to the house.

Pulling up by the front door he spoke curtly.

'You'll need to change. We both will. We're wet through. And have your mother tend to that arm wound.'

To be fair, he did open my door and support me as I stepped down but that was it. I glanced at the icy expression on his face under his hood. Whatever affection he'd had for me was gone.

We loped across the few feet of slushy

190

puddles to the front door. Ryan had parked as close as he could to the ranch house, leaving the engine idling away.

Sheltered by the porch, I was trembling and my teeth chattering so loudly, I thought they'd break. The white yard we'd left maybe thirty-five minutes earlier was awash with grey. Visibility through the downpour was maybe a few hundred feet.

Mom opened the door.

'What's happened?' Then she saw the state of me. Ryan explained what happened.

'She needs a hot shower, Rhonda. Me as well. I'd prefer her to have a lingering bath and stay here but not in her present state. She'll have to come with us. Emma too. Sorry, but we can't leave immediately. How's Barry?'

I felt so guilty. I'd forgotten about my daddy, too cold to even think straight.

'Hanging on in there. The delay might be a good thing; wash away more of the slippery snow and any black ice.'

She ushered us through the doors to

191

the bathrooms and fussed about finding fresh clothes for Ryan as she helped me undress. I'd only seen Emma once as I'd passed her in the hall, all dressed up for the cold and rain. I prayed that she wasn't too traumatised.

The shower and dry clothing helped arrest the shivering but, by the time we were in the Jeep, I was still chilled. We couldn't have the heater on high as Dad, semi-conscious on the back seat with my mom and Emma, was hot with the fever and breathing rapidly. Mom was talking to him as she mopped his brow with cold compresses.

That left me in the front with Ryan, himself changed and concentrating hard on the dangerous task driving through the torrential storm. The wipers were on high speed as we approached Fink's Ghost Creek once more. Huddled up, under Ryan's blanket and with a woolly hat on, I peered out the side window as we crossed the bridge. Dad's tractor was resting upright at the bottom of the slope, exactly where I'd been. Turning to Ryan,

I saw his face was pale. He'd seen where the tractor was too. The rocks under the wheels hadn't stopped it plunging to the bottom.

I tried to speak, but thought better of it. My harsh words from earlier couldn't be undone with platitudes, not when my father's life depended on Ryan's driving. One slip in his concentration and we might crash again.

All the time, we were tense, wanting the trip to be complete and my father rushed to emergency care. The sweeping gusts of rain were relentless. Twice the vehicle lurched dangerously close to the soft, grass edges, blown by side winds.

I felt my arm wet and sticky in the new clothes. It was still bleeding, maybe due to the anticoagulants I'd been on. Mom's expert bandaging had only done so much. If the others noticed, they said nothing.

Soon the windswept branches and grasses gave way to houses as we negotiated the suburban streets and roads of

T-Town. There was far less traffic than normal.

Street lights in the middle of the day guided us to the emergency entrance of Hillcrest Hospital South. Ryan pulled up undercover, jumped out and returned with two orderlies and a young intern. I watched as they wheeled Dad in, holding Emma close to me. Ryan was close to exhaustion from the stress and his own ordeal but refused any contact with me.

'I'll park up and see you both inside, Amber. You best get that arm seen to. I just hope Barry will be all right.'

'You did all you could, Ryan. Thank you,' I said, reaching out to at least shake his hand. He didn't move, except to say he'd best move his vehicle in case an ambulance arrived.

'See you inside, then,' I said, rain splashing at our feet.

Emma and I watched as he climbed in and left. We went to a waiting room where about a dozen people were seated. I was surprised there weren't more, given the continuing dangers outside. Mom was there, Dad having already been admitted.

'I gave them your details, too, Amber, about your op and all. They're getting your file from your hospital.'

'Thanks, Mom.' I didn't have the patience or strength to cope with reception.

Emma snuggled up to me. She hated being around lots of strangers and buried her face in my coat. It was horrible to put her through this.

'Have they said anything about Daddy yet?' I inquired of my mother.

'Give them a chance, Amber. This is the best place, though. Doctor Hussain is on the job. He's the expert for septicaemia.'

'That's definitely what it is, then?'

'Yes. Bacterial as I thought rather than fungal. Doctor Hussain has had a drip of IV antibiotics set up. At least it's not sepsis and his blood pressure hasn't dropped. Now, it's a waiting game. Your dad has the constitution of a grizzly.

195

He's strong and he's tough. That's in his favour.'

I held her hand until a nurse came to fetch me. The checks on my BP and heart were thorough and bloods were taken yet again. The wound was cleaned properly and I was told to wait in reception. Outside, the blizzard had returned with a vengeance. We'd been lucky to get here while the temperature was above freezing.

'Crazy weather,' she commented.

'Sure is.' The Green Skies above the clouds would be responsible for the yo-yo temperature fluctuations, of that I was certain. One of the keywords in my paper was 'unpredictability' and this was certainly the case now.

'So much for the darn forecast on telly. He said it would clear up.'

'He?' I asked her, sensing the response.

'That Lachlan guy. He virtually guaranteed it.'

'Actually, I'm a chief meteorologist from Galveston. I can tell you this is our future for a few days, nurse. Lightning, high winds ... possibly twisters. It's the Green Skies causing it.'

'If that's the case, Miss Devane, some-one should be warning us folks. I means us Okies seen our fill of bad weather, but not as bad as this. The odd tornado, but not as many as OKC.'

It was true. Oklahoma City did get more than its share of Tornado Alley twisters. But T-Town wasn't a stranger to them, especially this time the year. We had a tornado shelter under the ranch house — Gran's Fraidy Cat Shelter. Even young Emma knew what to do if we thought one was coming.

'You're absolutely correct,' I agreed. 'Your weather girl, Madison, has been trying but she was sacked this morning. Seems like this Lachlan Peabody doesn't want folk to hear the truth.'

'That's just terrible. Can't you do anything? I mean, I read your notes, I understand you're not well but can't you help us — please?'

'I'll try,' I said. At least I could con-tact Chuck. Just one phone call. After all, I had my own family to look after first.

* * *

Ryan was sitting there when I returned. The blood was still there on my clothing but the arm was disinfected, cleaned and bandaged. Emma was solving a maze puzzle in a book.

Mom looked up. I gave her a reassuring smile.

'What about Dad?' I asked, sitting on the opposite side to her from Ryan and Emma. He hadn't made any effort to shift up for me and, from his expression, he wasn't interested in starting a conversation.

'Stable. It's seeming like we got him here on time. He's conscious but weak. It'll take awhiles for the antibiotics to kick in.'

'That is a relief. Can we see him?'

'Not right now, Amber. He's resting and they're doing tests. They'll tell us when.'

I nodded, reaching across Mom to Emma. She smiled at me, clearly more relaxed with Ryan taking time to play with her.

'Where did you get the book from, Emma?' I wondered.

'Ryan bought it me, Mommy. He's nice.' She and he returned to the page she was drawing on.

'Thanks, Ryan,' I said to him.

'I did it for Emma,' he replied matter-of-factly. The inference was that he didn't do it for me. I chewed my lip. He was hurt and there was no way I could blame him.

'Even so, thanks,' I muttered. Mom seemed oblivious to us. She had her own concerns.

Ryan spoke up, glancing at me.

'She shouldn't be here, Amber. Can't you see that she's stressed? We can let you both know when we have news.'

He was right, of course. But if not here, then where could we go? Ah – Maddy's place wasn't far, according to the address I'd written down.

I agreed with him and said I'd try Maddy. Our cell phones were useless as far as signals went, even the figures on the display were wrong.

Excusing myself, I went to a pay-phone. We were not quite back in the Dark Ages, but not far off. From snippets of conversation around us, it was evident that Tulsa was virtually cut off from the outside world. Landlines were down in places while flights and train services were disrupted.

'Madison. Is that you? It's Amber,' were my first anxious words.

To welcome a four-year-old and cranky mother whom she'd only just met was expecting a lot, yet Madison was happy to help. It was extremely gracious of her, considering her trauma at work a few hours earlier.

'Should I come to collect you?'

'No. It's bad news out there. We'll grab a cab, thanks. See you in about twenty. And Maddy, thanks a million. You're a life-saver.'

'More than happy to help, Amber. I

just hope your daddy's gonna be OK. See you two soon.'

With that, she hung up.

Mom said she'd contact us at Madison's, the moment she heard any news about Dad. I gave her Maddy's home number. Ryan had gone to get a bite to eat and was intending to stay with my mother, at least for a while. His apartment wasn't far and, even if his car were snowed in again, a cab wouldn't take long.

I asked Mom to say goodbye from us, grateful that I didn't have to embarrass either of us by trying to be civil in person. I'd been in the wrong but now wasn't the time to discuss it.

Emma seemed pleased to be leaving the waiting room, which was now filling up with all sorts of weather-related injuries.

There was a vacant taxi outside, which was lucky. All around there was the special quiet that happens in a snowstorm. Unlike earlier, Emma wasn't impressed, complaining about the cold instead. We slid into the back seat, grateful that it was cosy and warm.

'Where ya, goin', ma'am?' the cabbie said, in a nasal New Yorker accent. I read it out to him and we started off.

Emma's eyes lit up a little when I showed her what was in my bag, especially as we'd be sleeping in strange beds at Madison's tonight.

'You brought Teddy,' she exclaimed. 'Can I have him now? Please, Mommy?'

'Of course.' I passed him over. It was a last-minute decision to bring him, though I'd forgotten all about him in the hospital. Tonight I was determined to spend time with Emma. I'd been neglecting her far too much, relying on my parents instead of taking on my responsibilities.

The roads were almost deserted. 'Been busy?' I called to the driver, who was uncharacteristically quiet for a cabbie from Brooklyn.

'No. Ya' dig? Most folks around here are stayin' in. Okay? Losers. Yuh with me? We get much wawhse blizzards where I'm from. Ya' dig?'

'Yes. I 'dig',' I replied and made sure not to ask any more questions. It wasn't far, fortunately. Even so, he was dead right about T-Town turning into a ghost town — without the tumbleweeds.

He pulled up as close to Madison's front door as he could. I gave him a generous tip. There's a saying about mad dogs and Englishmen enjoying the midday sun. The same could be said for mad huskies and New Yorkers when it came to snowstorms. We'd been lucky at the hospital. I'd not see one other taxi on the journey here.

Putting our hoods up, we went quickly to the front door. It opened before I could ring the bell. Madison was watching for us arriving. She took us through to the kitchen, boiling up the water in some strange jug with a lid on.

She noticed my curiosity. 'It's an electric kettle. I brought it back from England.'

'Never seen one,' I confessed. It was nothing like our kettles. In any event, she switched it off when we all decided that hot chocolate made with milk was called for. I asked Madison about her husband as we prepared the three drinks. Apparently, he was stuck in Seattle as, not only was our airport snowed in, they'd grounded planes due to the mysterious 'sky illness'.

Sitting down to chat while Emma and Teddy watched some cartoons, it was time to evaluate the situation with Maddy's job.

After she related the traumatic morning, being dismissed in public for disobeying Lachlan's wishes, I again mentioned contacting her absent 'proper' boss, Shirley.

'Is there any way to phone her to put her in the picture, Madison? Any clue at all?'

She mused deeply took a sip of the hot, sweet confection and furrowed her brow.

'Maybe. She told us all she'd be concentrating on some family emergency and couldn't cope with that and day-to-day television business. Later she confided that her married sister had offered to take on the job of caring for her mom after some health issues. Shirley had persuaded her not to, because her job as a politician was more important.'

That helped a little.

'Did she say her sister's name, at all?'

'It was a few weeks ago. Carol? Caroline? I don't know. Something like that.'

It was disappointing but it was something. As her sister was married, there'd be a different surname.

'Listen, Madison. Could you please keep an eye on Emma? I'd like to ring my chief in Galveston on your landline. I'll pay, of course.'

She dismissed my offer of money as we went to her study. 'One day it'll be a nursery but right now I guess I need to concentrate on finding a new job, especially if Shirley backs her boyfriend's decision.' She glanced at the clock. 'Getting late. I figure it's about time to do something to eat. OK if I ask Emma to help?'

I grinned. 'She'd love that. And

thanks again for everything. Mom said she'd ring with any news. I'll ask Chuck for a weather update since it's obvious anything Lachlan announces will be a fantasy.'

Maddy laughed at that.

'Yeah, that's for sure. Considering he's such a hotshot talk-show host, that guy doesn't have much on the internet to show for it. I did a Google on him, but the guy's a phantom.'

'Interesting. After dinner, maybe we can pursue that. When someone's like that, it means he's got things to hide, big-time.'

$\star$ $\star$ $\star$

My conversation with Chuck was enlightening. The Tulsa Met office had been sending accurate reports on the dire weather to the TV station yet it was apparently being ignored. Above the dense blanket of snow clouds, the sky above our county was a pastel green. Of course, no one noticed; the inhabitants were shielding their eyes from the snowy gales that whipped around their down-turned, hooded faces.

'Temperature fluctuations are dramatic, worse than anything I've seen. There are dry lightning storms on the edges of the static circle covering your terrain. In short, Amber, those Green Sky storms aren't budging. People need to be warned to take care.'

'You tried that, Chuck, as did a friend at the station. Not a great success. You were insulted, she was sacked. But we're trying to get it sorted. Trust me.'

Chuck took his role as director seriously. He believed in doing his best to forewarn people of the vagaries of the fickle weather that swept across our area of the states.

Even though he was concerned about me becoming involved due to my recent operation, I explained that it was well past that now. We discussed the best way forward. I explained, in detail, what had happened with Madison and that it was imperative that we contact the owner of the local television/radio station.

He scribbled down the facts and gave them to another member of the team who was a wizard with computer searches. He had my number here. Then I asked a question about the Tulsa office and explained my rationale. That was the one greatest thing about Chuck; he listened and was willing to support his team, whoever they were.

He once told me that he regarded himself as King Arthur with all of us Knights trusted to save the kingdom using our own special talents to follow our own quests. Although I questioned him calling me his Lancelot sometimes, I did acknowledge he was at his best co-ordinating from his round table in Camelot.

'Ideally I'd expect to see details of qualifications, Amber. However, we can do searches of our own and — bottom line — I trust your judgement.'

It felt great to hear him say that but I knew I could still screw things up.

Once again, I considered what I'd done to poor Ryan earlier today. All he had been doing was his best to help my family and save my dad. Hell, he wasn't a rancher. How could I blame him for driving into that ditch?

And yet, to my shame, I had. The ensuing trauma had broken us clean in two.

* * *

Not long after we finished our meal Madison got up to answer the phone, beckoning me over. It was Mom. I was so scared to hear what she might say.

'He's going to be all right, Amber. The antibiotics are working.'

I breathed a deep sigh of relief, wiping tears with the back of my hand.

'Thank the good Lord,' I told her. Calling Emma over, Gran explained that Grandpa was OK.

It was difficult for even me, her mom, to understand how much of the past weeks of drama had affected her. Every day I'd done my best to explain in terms she might understand. The sooner she

209

was at school, the better — if only for the interaction with kids her own age.

Mom said that he was now awake and hungry, although he was weak.

'They're keeping him in overnight at least and certainly tomorrow. They've set up a bed for me to stay with him.'

The advantages of being a well-respected member of staff, I thought.

'Is Ryan still there?' I wondered.

'Yes. He'll head home to his place later. Thank goodness that he wasn't up at the Observatory, though. It was damaged today according to him, despite nothing on the news. Some lightning strike. When I told him that I figured all big buildings had a lightning rod thingy, he explained that it was special lightning … a super …'

'A superbolt?' was my immediate suggestion, feeling my toes curl in fear.

'Yep. That's the word he used, Amber.' She paused, possibly realising the implications of the unreal weather on the past twenty-four hours.

'It's that Green Cloud problem, isn't

it? One of the nurses mentioned floods. Three inches of rain out Liberty way on route 75 since last night. No snow. Just rain. A deluge, she called it.'

We chatted a while longer, she more relaxed now that the worries about Daddy had abated. He wasn't out of the woods, I realised. Nevertheless it was very promising.

I bade her good night, requesting she contact me the following morning with an update. As a final thought, I asked her to speak to Ryan if she would.

'We had words when the tractor went off the road. Suffice to say, I said some horrible things to him, things that were wrong and hurtful and totally nasty. I want to apologise in person but now's not the time. Just say that I'm so, so ashamed and sorry. Could you do that, please?'

Mom seemed to understand and said she would speak to him. 'But let me tell you this for nothing, Amber,' she concluded. 'Ryan's a sensitive person. He's done nothing but help this family today.

If you've upset him because of that foul temper of yours ...' She left the rest unsaid and then muttered a curt good-night.

Great! As if I didn't feel bad enough already, here was my mother adding to my guilt trip.

She was right, though. Although I was usually well-behaved as a child, I had been a right little madam at times, taking my frustration and anger out on the nearest person or object when life had become too much. I hadn't done it in years. Trust Ryan to be in the firing line at the wrong time and place.

Madison had been at the far end of the room with Emma and must have heard it all, yet she was polite enough to avoid upsetting me more.

'Superbolts, eh, Amber?'

'Yep. Wrecked part of the observatory where Ryan works. No one injured.'

Superbolts were very rare, being up to a thousand times more powerful than the average lightning strike. They hit between November and February, gen-

212

erally over the ocean. The energy was staggering; between ten billion and a trillion watts of power.

To think they were striking around Tulsa was positively mind-numbing. Lightning rods were useless, being so much molten metal in the first ten-thousandth of a second. There was no walking away from one of them. We both were aware of the implications, realising once again that the fine people of our county needed warning.

* * *

I put Emma to bed after we'd both peeked out of her window at the winter wonderland of Maddy's back garden. The snow was falling vertically now, the winds having dropped. In the tangerine light of the street lamps, it was positively beautiful to behold.

I tucked her in after telling her a fairy tale. We had no books to read or even nightwear, having left home in a hurry. As for underwear and a change of clothing for us both, there was a small Wal-mart a hundred or so yards away. I'd set out in the morning. Maybe the snow would be gone. Maybe I'd need a sled and a team of huskies. Who knew? I certainly didn't and I was the so-called expert.

As I returned to the living area, Madison was putting the last of the dirty plates and pots into the dishwasher. She explained that she'd been on the phone to her stranded husband who had told her that Tulsa was largely a no-go area travel-wise. Even if he'd flown to OKC and wanted to hire a car, they'd put a block on travel to our county due to an unprecedented number of accidents from lightning strikes. Our poor little county was suddenly off-limits to all intents and purposes.

Sitting down at last, we chose to open a bottle of wine while we checked out Maddy's iPad for some background on Mr Peabody. As Madison had mentioned earlier, our Lachlan had a presence on the net, yet it went back just seven months. Before that, it seemed that Mr

Peabody had been Mr Nobody.

Immediately, that suggested he'd adopted a new identity ... or at least had chosen to use a different part of his name.

'How will we track him now?' Madison asked me, brushing her luxuriant, copper hair back from her right eye. She was quite despondent.

I had a suggestion.

'Chances are he's always wanted to be prominent in whatever he has done, and one thing that's hard to disguise is your face. There is a website where you can upload a photo and it then analyses facial characteristics — like they show on some police or spy programmes.'

Madison stared at me, her blue eyes wide open. 'Should I wonder why you would be aware of this website?'

'We all have our secrets, young lady. Let's simply say Lachlan wouldn't be the first man I've met who has been a lying rattlesnake and leave it at that.'

'Fair enough. We can take his profile photo from his *T-Town Tonight* chat show.

Another point — he always wears a cravat. Says it makes him appear even more sophisticated than he is.'

We exchanged glances and burst into laughter.

'You've never seen him prancing around the studio as if he owns the place, Amber. The English have the perfect term for him; 'pretentious prat'.'

I repeated it, mentally adding it to my list of insults. The trouble is, if you insult a person who doesn't understand what it means, it sort of defeats the purpose.

Within minutes, the website was beavering away on the uploaded photo. 'Look — it has a match. From 2018 ... and another,' Madison exclaimed.

'Might not all be him. We'll see in a minute.'

It was worse than watching paint dry, but the eighty-nine results gradually loaded up. A few weren't right but most were, complete with cravat.

'You might change your hair colour or grow a beard but vanity stays the same, Mr Peabody. Now, Maddy. Which should we choose first?'

My new-found friend licked her lips in anticipation. We both gasped as the details and website came into view.

Madison gave a broad smile as she savoured the moment and read the text. 'Oh my, Mr Peabody. Who's been a very naughty boy, then?'

9

Consequences

It was apparent that Lachlan had a multitude of other identities. He was a chameleon, changing names, faces and locations throughout the length and breadth of America.

Quite often he'd left his employment under a cloud and I don't mean a green one. Embezzlement, fraud, you name it.

Given his chequered past, we were both amazed he'd chosen to be a presenter on television. True, it was only on Tulsa telly and, on first glance, he appeared quite different to the alter egos sought after in other states; his hair colour and style were changed, and there were none of the various facial hair styles his previous incarnations had sported. Madison and I decided he probably thought himself so clever now, that he had no chance of being found out. Boy, would he be in for a shock.

We took screenshots and copious notes, gradually building up a timeline of his adventures. They went back until 2007 in Maine, when one Jeremiah Jones first hit the local headlines as inheriting a substantial estate from his long-lost aunt. Unfortunately for him, his forged documents were poorly done and the scam resulted in him being imprisoned. He'd seemingly learned from that, and had avoided capture ever since when things went pear-shaped.

It was going on nine when Chuck rang back with news. He'd approved my request for Madison to join the Tulsa Met Bureau if she so wished. Though it was part-time, it was hers if Shirl didn't overturn Lachlan's decision to dismiss her. I hadn't discussed it with her, nevertheless, it was the least I could do given that she'd put her job on the line to support the truth about what was happening to the weather in the area.

'The main reason I'm ringing, Amber, is to inform you that I've spoken to the head of the television station. Her sister is a Senator in Iowa. Once I contacted the Senator and apprised her of the situation, she gave me Miss Shirley Cassidy's number.

'The story is that's she's been incognito, helping their brother to get off his drug habit; some retreat in the country, not far from Atlanta. She'll be phoning you at ten-fifteen your time.'

'That's nine-fifteen Central Time. I'd better finish up, boss. Thank you.'

'My pleasure, Amber. Hopefully you ladies can get this mess sorted. It's imperative that people there are warned. Satellite imagery shows that the Green Skies situation is intensifying. I do realise you have your own health issues and you are on leave, but you are the best the NWS has there in Tulsa. Good luck.'

He was right. These past few weeks of self-pity and my upside-down health and social life were in the past. I should accept responsibility and get back to what I did best. It was high time to tell my fellow Oklahomans the facts, and pray that was enough to save them from the worst that this diabolical anomaly could throw our way.

I hardly had time to inform Madison about her new job with the Tulsa National Weather Service if she wanted, before Shirley Cassidy buzzed her on FaceTime. It was better than the phone as we had vision and could all hear one another comfortably. The cable internet hadn't been affected adversely by the Green Skies EM interference as yet.

Introductions were quickly made, then Shirley apologised for being out of touch these past few weeks. Her cell phone had been switched off. Chuck had used a landline at the rehabilitation retreat to contact her.

'Bring me up to speed, Maddy.'

Madison summarised the weather situation, then went on to relate her and Lachlan's differing stance regarding the right to inform the public.

'It came to a head this morning when he dismissed me and asked security to escort me out.'

To her credit, Shirley was like Chuck, a manager who listened.

'Is this true, Miss Devane?' she asked me.

'Obviously, I only met Madison yesterday and I'm not privy to what happened off-camera but I watched your boyfriend humiliate my superior, Professor Polanski, on his talk show. Also, I saw his blatant lies when he presented the weather this morning after sacking Madison.'

She thought for some moments before shocking us with her next statement.

'Maddy. Lachlan isn't in charge. We might be in a relationship but there is no way that I'd put my multi-million-dollar business in his hands while I was away.'

Madison blinked. 'But the email you sent?'

'Forged. It must have been convincing for Trevor to have relinquished control after I left him in charge. What you're saying Lachlan's done doesn't make sense, though. Surely he'd realise I'd find out on my return and, relationship or not, there would be no way I'd forgive him. I mean, he's cute and charismatic but that's all.'

'Actually,' I interrupted, 'Lachlan isn't who you might think he is. As for when you return, I doubt he considers the implications of what he does. He lives for the present and, if things catch up with him, he bails and makes a run for it. He's clever, but that's not the same as smart. Madison will send you details of Lachlan's other 'lives' now. It's best if you read them, check them out yourself, then ring us back. I'm sorry, really sorry. We both are.'

We ended the call and topped up our wine glasses as we waited. Before long, Shirley came back on and it was plain that she'd been crying. Also, there was barely-controlled anger.

'I feel like the most gullible fool in history. The mistakes I've made with that … *thing*. You've clearly devised a plan for what to do next. But it will need me. This time we're not giving Lachlan, or whoever he is, the opportunity to disappear.'

We agreed. Lachlan's selfish actions had put our county in jeopardy. Now it was payback time.

'How soon can you get back to Tulsa?' I asked.

'Eleven, twelve tomorrow morning? I'll fly to OKC tomorrow. My car is there.'

'Yes. That'll work. Here's what I have in mind. Lachlan goldarn Peabody won't realise what's happening until it's too late.'

10

The Confrontation

By Friday morning, the snow was mostly gone. The rain and wind hadn't, though. When I went to venture out on the short walk to the shops, my borrowed umbrella blew inside out immediately, almost taking me with it.

'Take my car, Amber,' Madison offered.

'Can't drive … the stitches. Probably haven't got the strength in any case.'

Emma and I needed fresh clothes and toothbrushes. Although Madison had kindly offered us clothes for our special trip to the hospital and television station, her clothes were far too large for my lovely daughter.

'I'll drive you both. You can shop, grab your showers, then change but we'll have to get a wriggle on, Amber.'

'Thanks.' We'd had breakfast and were

wearing yesterday's clothing. I helped Emma into her coat and rain boots. I really hated dragging her along.

The weather was better than last night in some ways. Nonetheless, I could see tell-tale flashes of lightning on the rain-shrouded horizon. Despite Madison having the wipers on high-speed, visibility was difficult. We were lucky there was undercover parking outside the store. A section was roped off and it wasn't difficult to see why. Part of the roof had blown off.

'In and out,' I told Emma. 'No time for window-shopping today, my precious.'

There weren't many shoppers. I assumed they had more sense than to be out in this foul storm.

'Hope Shirl will be OK driving up here,' Madison said as we hurried through the clothing aisles.

'Me too. We need her there in person when we go on air. Lachlan will try to stop us otherwise.' We could expose him ourselves if it came to a confrontation — but I, for one, couldn't deal with that on top of everything else.

I thought about it all happening in my life; Dad's infection, recovering from my op, Ryan and what might have been, and the responsibility of helping the populace of my home county prepare for what was to come. Oh yes, let's not forget that niggling inner sensation that all wasn't right with my heart, in spite of all those assurances to the contrary.

The shopping done, we all returned to Madison's home to prepare for the day ahead. Mom rang to update me on Dad. He was well and truly on the mend, complaining about being cooped up with chores to do back at the ranch.

I explained we'd be calling by to see him later, along with his fluff-bunny Madison. 'He'll like that, Amber. Perhaps when I tell him the crotchety ol' coot will settle down.' When I inquired about Ryan, she explained that he wasn't able to be there today. He was involved in assessing the damage out at Silver Springs.

'Did you explain I was sorry for my

outburst yesterday?'

'Yes. I told him, Amber.' Mom was holding something back; I could sense it.

'And?'

'And nothing. You're a grown woman, Amber Louise. Honestly. I declare. This lovers' spat you two had is something to figure out yourselves.'

Lovers' spat? Was that all it was? I wondered, feeling relief. As for being lovers — was I denying the facts that others could see?

* * *

The drive to the hospital was much more pleasant as both rain and wind were less severe. I was thankful for that. Dressed in one of Madison's dresses and a fetching sweater, I'd at least appear professional if — as planned — I were able to present my case.

For some strange reason, there had been no warnings from the Mayor or emergency services broadcast on KTUL Tulsa. It was the main television station in our city and its sister radio station was also up there as the most popular one to listen to. Had Lachlan's influential 'everything will be fine' attitude convinced the powers that be not to panic the citizens unnecessarily?

When we arrived at Reception, the person there directed us to a private room on the third floor. It did seem that staff like Mom were given special considerations in this place.

The door was open and Dad was propped up with pillows, chatting happily to Mom when we entered. Emma ran to them both. Dad's eyes then went to Madison.

'Tarnation, Rhonda. You weren't kidding. It's my favourite weather lady in the flesh.'

He was actually blushing. Madison gave him one of her most gracious smiles.

'So this is the man who thinks I'm a fluff-bunny? Pleased to meet you, Mr Devane. You too, Mrs Devane.'

Mom reached out to shake her hand.

'Rhonda and Barry, please.'

Dad, in turn, was now quite contrite.

'Er ... Sorry, Miss Madison. I just assumed that such a pretty lady wouldn't have smarts as well. I thought you were there just to brighten up the breakfast show with your beauty. Amber tells me that you're a proper meteorologist like her. It's a shame that she couldn't have been gorgeous as well as clever too.'

He grinned at me, then winced from moving too quickly with the drip in his arm.

'Dad,' I remonstrated with a playful punch. 'If I were you, I'd quit while I'm ahead.'

'Right after a photo with me and Miss Madison. The guys won't believe me otherwise.'

Madison laughed and gladly obliged, even giving him a peck on the cheek as Mom snapped away on her phone.

'You do realise she's happily married, Dad?' I reminded him.

'So am I, Amber. I wonder what else Madison and me have in common?' He gave her a wink, before breaking into a coughing fit.

Mom passed him some water. 'Serves you right, Barry Devane. And now, I figure you two ladies had better head over to the television station. From what Amber says, you have some pretty important messages to pass on to folks.'

Dad added his advice.

'And give that no-good Lachlan Peabody his comeuppance. Not before time, if you ask me.'

Emma had been watching it all while holding my hand, her smile showing how much she loved the friendly atmosphere.

I had a quiet aside with Mom.

'Dad's all right then?'

'He's his normal self, almost. By the way, you'd best leave little missy here with us. We'll look after her. You'll have your hands full with this Lachlan fellow, I reckon.'

I thanked her.

At that instant, the lights flickered and went out as blindingly bright flashes lit up the gloomy sky to the eastern side of town. A deafening thunderclap rolled over the building, making most of us cover our ears as everything shook.

I quickly calculated that the ten seconds between the flash and thunder meant it was about two miles distant.

We stared out of the window. Tulsa was in semi-darkness; well, apart from fires and sparks. Then after a short, tense silence, the hospital lights and monitors beeped back to life.

Most of the city was still without power.

'Superbolt?' Madison questioned me. 'Never seen one before.'

'Me neither,' I confessed, holding my trembling Emma close. Kneeling, I tried to reassure her.

'Just pray no one was injured ... or worse,' my mother said sincerely.

Chuck had told me there'd been injuries but no deaths reported. Still, that had been last night.

'Power station,' Dad said, peering out of the window to a plume of smoke beginning to rise from the flames. 'Check the television, please.'

Mom switched it on and flicked between channels. Blank screens stared back at us. If Madison's station was off-air then our journey there would be pointless. A picture appeared at last; KTUL was displayed in the top right corner.

'Seems like you'll have a captive audience, Amber and Madison,' Dad concluded. 'That substation won't be fixed any time soon.'

'No pressure, then,' I murmured. Although I'd mentally prepared what I had to convey and had visual aids and video footage with me, I felt sick as a pumpkin at Hallowe'en at the thought of speaking to hundreds of thousands of anxious viewers.

Realising my apprehensions, Mom and Dad reassured me.

Kissing us farewell, Dad mentioned that he was keen to get to the farm and check if everything was hunky-dory. Mom and I exchanged glances as I bit my lip. I wondered if the old tractor was still on the river bank, or halfway down the Arkansas River to the Mississippi.

* * *

We arrived at the QuikTrip store next to KTUL, where we'd arranged to meet in their fast-food kitchen. The plan was to finalise the attack strategy outside of the station, as Lachlan might have gotten wind of what we were up to otherwise.

Trevor McShane was already waiting at a table. Madison introduced us as he had no idea who I was. His next words were, 'What in the Sam Hill is going on?'

We gave the tall, well-dressed Texan a quick run-down on the deception perpetrated by Lachlan. He'd convinced Trevor that he'd been replaced as the man in charge of the station with some fancy talking and a number of what we now knew to be forged papers and emails.

Trevor was fuming when he heard that, using some choice words he'd learned as a trail-hand in his youth. Even I blushed. Finally, he simmered down enough to realise he'd overstepped the mark. He apologised profusely.

Just then, a very windswept woman in her early fifties entered the Kitchen, removed her scarf and waved in our direction. It was Shirley. I'd not noticed last night that she was a dead ringer for an older Jennifer Aniston. Madison beckoned her.

'Howdy,' I said, standing and extending a hand. 'Pleased to meet you in person.'

'Howdy, yerself, Amber. Before we start, I need me a drink.'

Madison called a waitress over. 'I don't think they serve alcohol, Shirl.'

'That's a shame. I could do with a tequila … a double. That drive from OKC was something else. Black coffee all around and keep it coming. And some of them fancy cakes over yonder.' She handed the girl two twenties. Clearly, she was a woman used to taking charge. While waiting, she took a moment to take off her jacket and recover.

'You weren't joshing me about this Green Skies stuff, Amber. I actually saw it up there through a break in the clouds while I was dodging lightning bolts about forty miles south of here. Lordy. Thought my number was up more than once.' Then she gave me the most amazing smile.

'Don't you worry none about speaking on my television station, Miss Devane. Me and Maddy here, we'll look after you when we're on-air. You being an expert and all, I was thinking of giving you a fancy title, catchy-like. What do you figure to Weather Witch?'

I must have looked horrified.

'No? Maybe not. Makes you sound like the villain of the situation, don't it? I'll give it more thought. Ah, here's our brain food arriving. Eat and drink up, my friends. We got a heap of planning to finalise. Zero hour is ...' She checked the clock on the wall. 'Forty-two minutes from now.'

* * *

Madison and I shared our dossier on the chameleon-like Lachlan Peabody with Trevor. He, like us, was amazed. It seemed 'Lachlan' was a master at manipulation to achieve whatever he wanted.

Shirley confessed that it would be easier to simply have him arrested with no need for this subterfuge. She was, however, a very bitter and hurt woman. Their love had been a sham to allow him some authority in the station. There were probably some age-old adages about a woman and revenge. Shirley could probably write a few new ones after today.

Her plan was simple. She wanted him publicly humiliated and arrested on camera. It would be a talking point for weeks to come. When I mentioned that her association with him as lovers might be brought up, she dismissed it.

'This won't be the first scandal I've been involved in, Amber, and won't be the last. I own this station; not some faceless group of penny-pinching bureaucrats. Anyway, didn't someone say that there's no such thing as bad publicity?'

'PT Barnum. Apparently,' Madison mused. 'I believe you'd prefer an earlier quote from Oscar Wilde though, Shirley. Knowing you as I do…'

'Go on, Maddy. Tell us.' Shirley smirked. I could tell she was relishing what was happening.

'*The only thing worse than being talked about is not being talked about.*'

The grin grew wider. 'Yep. That's me all right. Shall we go?' We all stood up. The weather outside was going to pale in ferocity before what was heading towards Lachlan.

What happened next, though, surprised me.

'Listen up, you folks. Sorry to interrupt yer eating. My name's Shirley Cassidy and I own KTUL. Just wanna give y'all the heads-up to be watching on that big-ol' telly over there at midday. We got us a humdinger of a show lined up for you. This lady, Amber, is a Weather Wizard and she and Maddy, our own weather presenter, they's gonna give y'all the low down on what's happening to Tulsa's strange weather. Tell your friends. Hell. Tell your enemies.

KTUL … Twelve o'clock today.' There was applause, gradually building up as we headed out. No doubt about it, Shirl was quite a show-woman. And we were all geared up for the battle ahead.

Then I felt a twinge in my chest. I grimaced.

'You OK, Amber?' Maddy must have noticed.

I touched my upper tummy, rubbing it around.

'Yeah. Probably that double-cream pineapple doughnut. Indigestion. Let's go.'

* * *

Trevor had gone ahead to brief the studio staff and set up the Met footage that we'd be using to illustrate our points. He was prepared with a phone video from Shirley if any staff were uncomfortable about disobeying Lachlan's instructions. Once we began the show, we were sure that Lachlan would turn up demanding we cease broadcasting. That's when

Shirley would make her presence known, along with some of Tulsa's finest in order to arrest him. It would all be on-air.

'Don't worry, Amber. I'll be there to take up the slack if you get too nervous.'

I took Madison's hand. 'Thanks. I don't think it's nerves. I simply don't feel that clever. Maybe I'm pushing myself too much.'

'I can do it all if you want, Amber. I don't want you getting sick on me.'

I was being a drama queen. Maddy simply wasn't the person Tulsa needed — not to start with, anyhow. She could follow up, but if things went wrong, I should be the one up front. It was my research and my predictions. The viewing audience needed an authority figure to believe and sadly too many would dismiss Maddy just like Dad had, as just an air-head weather girl. That would change, but this ... this was my day.

The scheduled *Noon-Time With Nanette* was about to begin. Maddy and I were off-camera in the wings, having had a quick make-up session. Our radio microphones were online but conversations between us weren't on air.

'You ready, Amber? Just walk on with me but watch the cables and such. And don't forget; when the camera's on there's a red light, but try to talk to me or Nanette rather than the camera. We want people to be informed but not panicked.'

I nodded. My throat was dry so I took a gulp of water.

Nanette was on-air. 'Howdy, folks. Instead of beginning with our cookery section today, we have a special announcement regarding this horrendous weather we've all been having in T-Town and hereabouts these past few days. Therefore, I'd like y'all to welcome our own weather guru, Madison Baxter — along with the deputy head of Galveston Weather Bureau, Amber Devane.' There was no audience to clap but Nanette and the assembled floor and backroom staff did their best to welcome us.

I forced myself to smile while looking

ahead and avoiding tripping up. We all shook hands and Maddy sat, indicating where I should, by her side.

'Firstly Amber. What's going on up there above the clouds?'

'Green Skies, Nanette. Some of your viewers have probably seen them before the rains and snow came. There are changes going on that are causing extreme and very erratic weather. I did a paper on this a few years ago. It has happened before, though it is extremely rare.'

I sat back, relaxing into the prepared leading questions which Nanette was feeding me.

'I believe we have satellite photos of Tulsa, Amber. Could you talk us through them, please?'

Damn. I should have introduced them but the anchor-lady knew what she was doing, helping guests relax.

I could see that our faces had disappeared from the monitor. There on the screen was the southern part of the US with weather patterns sweeping across from left to right. All except for a green area over us. It stayed static as the twenty-four-hour loop repeated. Maddy pressed a button on her remote that she used when doing the breakfast weather and the green dot became bigger. I continued to elaborate as we watched tiny lightning flashes all over the green, pointing out the alternating snow and rainstorms as the satellite images zoomed in.

The camera switched back to us. 'That's all very fine, Amber but why should we take heed of your warnings? You're from the NWS in Galveston. Texans always say things are bigger there.'

I laughed politely, wincing as I did so. Something wasn't right. Maddy took up the slack as I paused to catch my breath.

'Amber's one of T-Town's locals; born and raised in Crescent Moon, just southwest of here. She cares for this county. That's why —'

The studio doors burst open at that point and a very irate Lachlan burst in on the set.

'Stop this travesty! Immediately!' he

screamed in a piercing voice. His face was red, his nostrils flaring. Mr Peabody was not a happy man.

The production team pretended to comply but the entire proceedings were continuing to go out live, no matter what he wanted.

'Maddy. What are you doing there? I sacked you for disobeying me.' His voice was even more shrill, now he thought we weren't on-air.

'She's with me,' I said as calmly as I could. I was the one in control.

'And who the dickens are you?'

'Amber Devane. You met my boss from the NWS a few nights ago. I'm here to explain about the weather to the viewers.' I gave him a condescending smile and sat back on the settee.

'What weather, you stupid woman? Everything's fine out there. A little shower, that's all. Now get off my show and out of my station.'

No one moved. I sat forward but made no move to stand.

'Not until you tell me who you are,

mister? Who you *really* are.'

He paused, making eye contact for a second.

'Me? I'm Lachlan Peabody. I'm in charge. This is all mine.'

He waved his arms widely, pausing when he noticed a camera trained on him. The red light was on.

'I gave you an order, Trevor. Turn it off. I'm your boss.'

The producer didn't budge from his console.

I sat back again, smirking.

'Oh, you're Lachlan Peabody, the charismatic talk show host? I'm sorry. You look so much like some other men the police in five other states regard as a person of interest. Names like Roland Cathcart, Joe Wilson, Keith Gold. The resemblance is remarkable, even down to that ostentatious cravat you prance around in.'

Throughout, there'd been wanted posters and other police documents shown on the monitors and on TV screens all around Tulsa.

Lachlan's ranting had ceased as he watched his cavalcade of prior identities revealed to the world. Recovering, he realised he might still bluff his way out of the corner he was in.

'Lady. I'm in charge. Now get out. Take that Maddy woman with you.'

I nodded to the control booth. Out of the shadows, Shirley appeared.

Lachlan reacted quickly, instinctively trying to save his miserable skin.

'Shirley, my love. Thank goodness you're here. You should hear the slanderous insul — '

'Save your breath, Lachlan or whoever you pretend to be. Officers from the Tulsa Police Department are here and will arrest you for forgery and misrepresentation, to begin with. My lawyers will decide on other charges.' She crossed the floor to sit by Maddy and me as two burly men in uniform led a devastated Lachlan away, screaming abuse.

She patted my arm, whispering 'Well done.' I breathed a sigh of relief. It was hard to believe that I'd done that.

Shirley then took control of the programme. She was excellent at assuring the audience that the poor reporting of weather on KTUL was finished. She took full responsibility but subtly made it clear that Lachlan was the evil usurper who had seized control of her treasured KTUL in her absence.

'He's going away for a long time, my friends, and I promise you that I won't let you down again.'

I felt the pain in my chest, stronger this time. It wasn't going away. I had to continue, though.

Shirley handed the programme back to Nanette, retreating to watch the proceedings continue. We all had a message to get out there, didn't we?

'How long will this Green Skies phenomenon last, Amber, and what can we expect to happen?'

It was awkward to focus. I blinked.

'Sorry ... Can I have a drink, please?'

One of the staff brought a glass of water though it didn't help much. I spilt some on my chin, my hands trembling.

Facing the camera, I dabbed a tissue on my face.

'You have to realise I'm no fortune-teller. I'm a forecaster but this ... this is so unprecedented. However, it will change. Best guess another week. Maddy? Could you please explain?'

I was finding it hard to concentrate ... to breathe. Maddy was content to take over and the director focused on her, allowing me to sit back and try to regain my composure.

I only half-heard her explaining what we figured would happen. The snow and rain would disappear simply because the Green Skies was a closed system, unable to assimilate any moisture from the other weather patterns sweeping by Tulsa County. The mad temperature changes, lightning and winds would continue but we'd now have tornadoes to contend with, far more than normal.

Shirley passed me another cup of water from off-camera, whispering to inquire if I were OK. I nodded, took a mouthful and forced myself to be as strong as I could be. My last words had to be said by me – the so-called expert.

I spoke when Maddy had finished.

'Folks. We're all Oklahomans in this together. There is no need to panic-buy goods because it's the end of the world. Y'all are better than that. Now that you folks realise what we're all up against, we can survive. The lightning and torna-does? Hell. We're used to that. If things look bad, we do what we've always done — protect ourselves and our families and help our neighbours. Oh, don't forget what my dear old granny called the Fraidy-Cat Shelters under our homes. They're not just for tornados, you under-stand.'

Nanette began to thank Maddy and me, but I just remembered.

'Sorry, Nanette. One final thing.' Things were becoming hazy and the pain was getting awful bad but I had to smile and say this. 'You folks can take control by sending reports here to KTUL or the NWS in Tulsa. We have email and phone numbers coming on the screen. Video reports, or just telling us what's happening in your... neck of the woods. That's ... all I have to say.'

Nanette took control again as I shuddered, hopefully off camera. Aware that I was struggling, Maddy helped me to stand up, as did Shirley.

'We need a doctor here,' Maddy said to the staff. My whole body was on fire, the pain in my chest becoming ... 'Quick. She's collapsed,' I heard someone yell. 'Call 911. She needs — ' I felt my body stop. What was happening?

11

Aftermath

It was like waking from a very deep sleep when you couldn't remember where you were or what you were doing there. At first, it was the distant sound of voices, then the soft texture of material against my skin. Opening my eyes was hard, a bright light overhead forcing me to blink a number of times. Then I felt the dull ache in my chest.

'About time you woke up, sleepyhead. You had some of us worried.'

My head hurt and I felt so groggy.

'Where …?' I croaked like some swampland bullfrog.

'Your hospital. Even gave you your old room … well, almost.'

Only then did I recognise the voice. Ryan. I turned my head, trying to focus.

'What …?'

'We're not playing twenty questions,

251

Amber. I shall try to explain what happened, or what they told me happened.' He pulled his chair closer, leaning over me, smiling.

'You had a funny turn at the telly station after your brill job explaining what's going on. To begin with, they figured you overdid it too soon after your operation. Maddy told them the hospital where you'd been treated. Good thing too.'

He paused as a nurse entered to check my vitals and the drip. 'You were right about your heart, but it's all fixed up now. They put a stent in. You can't move until the small incision heals.'

'They didn't cut my chest open?' I pulled down my hospital gown to examine the area. Ryan turned away, a little uncomfortable. Not that he could see anything.

'No. Angioplasty. Went in through your femoral artery, they said.'

'Oh.' That explained the dressings down there that I'd just noticed.

'Being you, Amber, you had something unusual in your heart. It was intermittent so they had problems working out what was wrong with you … apart from your temper.'

Was he being sarcastic? Had I hurt him that much? I turned back to gaze into his eyes.

'Ryan. I was wrong to say what I did to you. Totally. No excuses. I … sorry, I said no excuses. You've shown nothing but kindness and love to me and Emma … Emma! Where is she? Is she OK?'

'Relax. She and your parents are just taking a break from their vigil by your bedside. I told them I'd keep an eye on you. Your dad is fine, though still fuming at you about the tractor, I think.'

'Me? I wasn't driving. Why would he blame me?'

Ryan broke into a broad grin. 'Gotcha.'

Cheeky chipmunk. But at least the ice was broken between us.

'Are you saying that I'm forgiven for my idiotic outburst?' The nurse was still there, unobtrusively doing something with the drip. 'Amber. I love you. I don't blame you for saying that I tried to kill you.'

'You should have. I was expecting too much from you, to steer something you'd never driven before in those conditions.'

The nurse gently interrupted. Her name tag said *Josie*.

'Excuse me, Miss Devane. I need to examine the incision. You're on anticoagulants and there might be some bleeding under the dressing. It might be better if your friend …?'

'Oh, goodness. For sure,' Ryan stammered. 'I'll wait outside.'

As he stood to leave, I took his hand. It was so strong and warm. 'Aren't you going to give me a goodbye kiss, Ryan?'

'I'll only be a few minutes,' Josie told me.

'That's good. When he comes back, I can give him a hello kiss too.'

Ryan didn't have to be prompted any more. It wasn't lingering and passionate but it was perfect. The hello kiss, once the nurse was gone, would be much more private.

With Ryan outside and the door closed, I was examined and told it was healing well.

'Sorry about just now, Josie. It's something I needed to do. Should have done it days ago but it was this heart thing. I was petrified to commit.'

'As your boyfriend explained, you're fine now but you'll have to take it easy. What you did — on the television — I wanted to say thanks from all of us in T-Town.' That cheered me up, no end. 'Also, for when he returns, there's some toothpaste and perfume in the top drawer. I can get them if you like. And a quick brush of your hair might help as well. Just don't go moving too much until we're satisfied that incision won't open up.'

I accepted gratefully. After she finished and my mouth no longer felt like a trash can, I asked Josie what the weather was like today — assuming that it was day. She opened the inbuilt metal shades between the two window panes.

'Grey, misty. Not much wind. Is there

a special name for this in your weather-world, Amber?'

'There is.' I looked at the fine droplets on the glass. 'It's called 'mizzle' — a mix of drizzle and mist. Very depressing. What time is it?'

'About two p.m. Why?'

My mind tried to make sense of that. I was recalling semi-lucid moments in the ambulance and at the hospital. The operating table too. I was supposedly awake when they did the angioplasty. They couldn't have done all that in an hour and a half since the broadcast, surely?

'And the day?'

'Why, Sunday, of course. You've been here two days. No end of visitors. Even the big boss of KTUL and your little girl, of course, just to reassure her. You were awake. Don't you remember?'

'Vaguely,' I replied. Two days?

'The twilight anaesthetics sometimes play tricks with your memories. They cause anterograde amnesia that means you don't form memories of what happened during the operation and afterwards.'

That made sense. They would have relaxed me in addition to reducing the pain, I guessed.

Josie covered me up again, fluffed the pillows then returned my toiletries to the drawer. I felt much more human and thanked her.

'That boyfriend of yours. He's virtually always been around. You're one lucky lady.'

'Yeah. I guess I am. You're sure I'm OK now, though ... medically?'

'That's what they tell me. Your heart consultant will be in later. He'll explain.'

As she left and Ryan re-entered, I understood how right she was. What was that song by that Australian singer from the Eighties, before I was born? *I Should Be So Lucky*.

Ryan came over slowly as I waited expectantly, trying to appear enticing in the most unattractive nightwear I could imagine. Even that tatty nightie that he'd seen me wearing the first snowy night, was positively ravishing compared to this garment with the name of the hospital printed all over it.

The warm hand on my cheek and the depth of his dark eyes as his face came closer made my skin tingle. This was going to be the best hello kiss ever. Our lips touched lightly at first, then he drew back, teasing me before another touch at a different angle, more sensual this time. He paused again, brushing a strand of hair from my ear.

'I love you, Amber,' he whispered, his breath warm as he nuzzled my ear lobe. My breath caught in my throat at the sensation and I sighed in anticipation. Then he kissed my cheekbone and the tip of my nose before returning to the lips. He didn't draw back.

It was heaven. Absolute heaven.

* * *

Later, as we awaited the return of my family, Ryan asked me why the change of heart about him … about us?

'Lying in a hospital bed gives you time to think. After counting the number of screws in the window frames so many times, you turn your thoughts inwards. I'm not talking about this hospital visit, but the last time when I was by myself so much of the time.

'Back then, I was angry at Joshua dumping me and Emma, and it depressed me. Then there was the unfairness of the cancer. Negative emotions consumed me and even at home, then meeting you again, the hatred was there, eating away.'

Ryan clenched then opened his hands, staring at the nails. His head remained lowered.

'Believe me, Amber. I understand anger ... frustration, self-loathing ... loss.'

'You do. I only wish I'd been there to comfort you as you have me,' I told him, reaching out with my free hand to take his. It was so strong yet gentle and vulnerable also. Lifting it to my lips, I kissed the back, then held it to my cheek.

'You might not have been there, yet Barry and Rhonda were. Still doesn't explain why you've allowed me into your life, so suddenly.'

'No, I guess it doesn't.' I giggled a little. It was so difficult to explain. I had to try, though.

'As I told you, I was afraid that there was something wrong with my heart and it wouldn't be fair to involve you. I loved everything about you but refused to admit it to myself, or you. Then there was the Green Skies distracting me. There was a conflict about my work responsibilities and simply letting myself float off into a 'happy ever after' fairy tale life with you.

'I haven't been conscious much since they brought me here from the studio but I heard your voice in my head.' I blushed. 'You were there in my dreams as well. Emma too. The three of us in some ideal future. Waking up just now, things were clear. It was you I wanted more than anything as my partner... as my husband.'

'Whoa, Amber. I never said anything about marriage. But if that's a proposal ...?' His dark eyes glowed with mock outrage, then amusement. His fingers touched mine tenderly.

We sat there quietly again; gazing at the grey mist outside and each wondering about our future. Like me, I sensed Ryan was apprehensive about the weather. It was a momentary calm again as the Green Skies adjusted its method of attack. To me, it seemed almost like a living wild beast attacking our beloved country.

'It's coming back, isn't it, Amber? An onslaught. Maddy explained it when she came to visit you, while you were asleep. She's been on KTUL informing the county that today shouldn't lull us all into thinking that it's over.

'By the way, she said no one has been killed, there's just massive property damage from the storms and flooding. Those warnings of yours worked a treat.'

'That's a relief.'

Even so, the damage? It was sad.

'What's next, then?' He was stoic in his attitude. Most Oklahomans were. We'd had many tornadoes in the past and would in the future too.

'The self-contained cell around the Green Skies has run out of moisture and energy. That's why today's a 'mizzle day'. No winds but the last remnants of the rain falling. Tonight, maybe, definitely tomorrow, the winds will regroup as the temperature gradients become bigger. It might be eighty in Broken Arrow but twenty here, and wind flows from warm high pressure to cold low pressure. The lightning will start up again, along with tornadoes. Lots of them.'

Ryan nodded. 'That's pretty much what Maddy told us. She's been quoting from your paper on the Green Skies. The satellite photos indicate that the green area is the same size as earlier last week and stuck in the same place over us. Transport in and out is better, but not by much. No flights at all.'

Just then my family knocked and entered the room. They would have been told that I was fine after the small heart operation, and had probably taken a long lunch to give Ryan and me some privacy.

It was a pleasure to find Dad appearing so chipper – but even better to witness Emma's smiling face.

'What? No hug and kiss?' She hesitated. 'I'm much better, sweetie. Hugs and kisses are exactly what the doctor said I needed.'

Emma came over and cautiously gave me both.

'Seems to me, Emma's not the only one following doctor's orders,' Dad smirked at Ryan, indicating the smudge of lipstick on his mouth. Mom gave him a playful nudge.

'Tush and nonsense, Father. Don't go showing the poor boy up.'

Dad playfully rubbed his arm where she touched him. 'I remember when you and me used to kiss, Rhonda. Last one musta been ... oh, way back in 'ninety-nine. It was a mighty fine one if'un I recollects correctly-like.'

He turned to Ryan. 'As for you, young Ryan, I hope your intentions are honourable. Hate to have to get out my shotgun and fetch the preacher.'

'Dad! Give us a chance at least. What do you think we've been doing here? I'm in bed, for goodness' sake.'

The stares from everyone apart from dearest Emma made me reconsider that imprudent statement. Time to change the subject. I blurted out the first thing I could think of.

'Well, it's great to see you're not too angry at us for the tractor at least.'

Dad's face suddenly went from jovial to serial-killer. Mom and Ryan were waving their hands frantically behind his back and making shushing gestures with fingers on lips. It was then that I guessed they hadn't broken the bad news.

'What have you done with my Samantha, Amber?'

Sensing an escalation of emotion in the room, Mom ushered Emma out of earshot. Looked like I'd really kicked a hornet's nest.

Crumbs. Which one was Samantha? The new one or the old?

Samantha Steiger? Yeah, Dad liked his alliteration. I took a punt.

'Oh, Samantha's fine. Totally dead — the battery that is — but she's fine.'

His face softened momentarily. I breathed deeply. 'The other one, the Massey-Ferguson? Er ... Not so much.'

'Marigold? My dearest, sweet little Marigold.' What was it with men naming machinery after women? I wondered, remembering the dumb tractor's soubriquet at last. My father often boasted about taking Marigold out for the day, trying to make Mom jealous.

Ryan stepped up to the plate.

'Barry. Marigold is a bit dirty, that's all. I drove it into the creek accidentally while trying to save your life. Your neighbour, Clarence, pulled it out and towed it. It's back in your shed.'

Dad's anger was there, yet it was tempered. 'Firstly, 'it' is a 'she' — and secondly, I didn't realise you could drive a tractor, Ryan.' Ryan was standing contrite like a naughty schoolboy outside the principal's office.

'Actually, I can't, Barry. That's why Amber and I went down the bank into the water. Amber almost died — '

Then Ryan straightened himself up, defiantly.

'Barry. You do realise that we had to go through hell to save your life? There was that blizzard, and we needed the tractor to tow my Jeep back to your ranch, then drive you into town. Amber wasn't up to going outside into that blizzard and then the tractor — your precious Marigold — almost crushed her. I hate to say it, my friend, but you need to get your damned priorities right. Amber almost died twice, as did you. A bit of dirt on your tractor? Grow up, Barry. You're better than this.'

Ryan's voice was low yet intense. Dad was about to yell back at him but stopped. Then the tears came.

'I'm sorry, everyone. I didn't realise what you must have endured. I was out of it, big time. And I swear I never meant to kick off like that. Can you forgive me for being a silly old fuddy-duddy?'

Ryan clapped him on the shoulder and

gave him a man hug. Me, I was more circumspect. Ryan's logic contrasted with my dad's shallowness. Nevertheless, my father rarely behaved like that so I decided to make some concessions. Besides, hadn't I behaved just as badly with Ryan?

'Dad. You're only in your fifties. 'Silly' and 'fuddy-duddy' I can live with. Figure you'd best fetch Emma and Mom back. And dry your eyes. I think you'd better apologise to them as well. What we've all been through recently — this weather — these Green Skies. They're taking their toll on us physically and mentally, and it's not over yet. We all have to stick together as a family, and that includes Ryan. After all of this is over, maybe you can show him how to drive a tractor properly?'

He nodded. Then he left to find the others. They were probably in the café.

'What was that about, Amber? I have never seen Barry behave like that. You don't think …?' Ryan stared out of the window. There was a green tinge to the clearing sky.

'Yeah. It's a possibility. The electro-magnetism screwing up our body chemistry might mess with our brains and emotions. It was in my paper — '

'I know. I read it. It … er, it might explain your reactions down at the creek too, accusing me of trying to kill you. Perhaps you should tell Maddy to include mentions in her daily weather update?'

'No way, Ryan. You might see it as warning people to watch out for odd behaviour in people around them and make allowances for it, but I've had a chance to think things through over the years. If anyone chooses to do something bad like assault then claim it was from the Green Skies, it'd be a get-out-of-jail-free card.

'No siree. People are going to be responsible for their own actions and my Green Skies will have nothing to do with it. I'll testify to that in court, too. As for the creek? Like I told you, there are no excuses for what I said, not even green ones.'

He stared at me for a moment. 'Whatever you say, my darling.'

* * *

The specialist came to talk to me after everyone had headed off to their respective homes. Reading my book wasn't all that easy lying flat on my back. The rain had vanished leaving me with a view of a cloudless, pale green sky.

'Howdy, Professor Allen,' I greeted him.

'Howdy yourself, Miss Devane. How are you feeling?'

'OK. A bit sore, but much better knowing that my heart's sorted.'

He checked my vitals on the monitors then used his stethoscope. Sensing a reticence to engage in conversation, I checked with him again.

'I am fine, aren't I, Doc?'

'Sorry, Amber. Yes, you are one hundred per cent. Tickety-boo, as my grandad used to say back in London. I was simply mentally giving myself a kick for not realising your problem earlier.'

He straightened up before making some notes on my chart.

'Doctor Calinich did ask for me to check your ECG results when you came in earlier last week. I should have been more thorough, but with the influx of plane passengers...

'When they brought you in from the television station on Friday, we did another ECG. You were in pain. I thought it might be microvascular angina, or cardiac syndrome X as it was referred to. Turned out I was wrong. You, my dear, had a very unusual condition. It's intermittent — was. I only picked up on it when I examined that long trace from the ECG done the other day.'

I relaxed. It hadn't been my imagination.

'By the way, you best get a decent sleep. Tomorrow looks like a busy day for you and a quieter one for us.' He gave me a wry smile.

'Care to elaborate, Professor?'

'When we discharge you, we shall not

have so many well-wishers ringing to enquire after your health. Passing out on that show gave you quite a high profile, Amber. I believe your friend Maddy is collecting you to take you to the studio for a weather update on that same show.'

'Oh great,' I moaned. 'Don't suppose you can keep me in here for another few days?'

'Sorry, Amber. We only treat sick people. Just sign this for me and I'll be on my way.'

He passed me a blank sheet of paper. 'What's this?'

'Autograph. For the missus,' the Professor admitted. 'She's been pestering me all day.'

12

Twister

I was given the all-clear to move around the following morning. That meant a decent shower and lots of phone calls.

Maddy arrived early with clean clothes and another dress and sweater from her already depleted wardrobe. She wanted me to appear my best on Nanette's programme.

I'd watched her on the breakfast show while I sat in the hospital café having a large breakfast. Although I was slowly regaining the weight I'd lost, I was still conscious of my gaunt, drawn face.

I was pleased to see a different woman presenting the weather.

'Let's go to Madison for a comprehensive weather round-up from the county, especially the latest on the Green Skies,' the anchorman said.

'Madison? My. How you've changed,'

I muttered, tucking into some pancakes and maple syrup. Maddy, the fluff-bunny with the revealing skirt and banal patter was gone. Madison, the confident, mature expert had arrived, and she was shining.

The normal minute-long report that skimmed over the forecast was transformed into comprehensive coverage with photos from viewers, highlighting the damage caused by the storms but also showing the most spectacular of skies and bizarre weather formations. Madison explained them all, continually asking for more feedback and where it had taken place.

Knowing that she was passing all info to the NWS meant vast quantities of data, but equally a chance to study the Green Skies Scenario in detail. If and when it happened again, the world would be ready.

Madison pre-empted my appearance on Nanette's show after her warnings about the weather today. No 'sunny with a chance of showers' for Tulsa county today, she told the viewers. 'High, unpredictable winds with tornadoes. Get yourselves prepared. And keep tuned to KTUL for regular updates and our special Tornado Watch warning, on both our station and our sister radio network.'

I was genuinely impressed and told her so when she arrived to take me from the hospital. I changed into the clothes she'd brought me and she helped me to her car, the wind destroying any sign of my attempts to make my hair presentable.

As we drove the few miles to the station, I expressed disappointment that she hadn't accepted the job at NWS Tulsa that I'd arranged. True, it was only part-time but with her qualifications, she'd have been a great asset.

It was a selfish wish. I'd virtually decided to move up to Tulsa from Galveston, and working with Madison would have been the ultimate Dream Team.

She turned from looking at the road, puzzled, before concentrating again on avoiding the rubbish and trash cans blowing across the street. Very few people were around. Those that were on the streets were struggling to stay upright.

'Of course. You haven't heard, Amber, being laid up in bed and all. Shirl and I came to a mutually beneficial arrangement after Lachlan was arrested. She was so apologetic at how he'd taken over the station in her absence, feeding her lies whenever she'd rung to check on things. I am now a 'weather expert' rather than a weather girl. I work at KTUL part-time and, mainly in the afternoons, work at the NWS. It's win-win for everyone, especially me.'

'Wow. Big wow. Then why do you need me on Nanette's show? I saw the job you did this morning — polished and professional.'

'Amber. You're the expert on Green Skies. I've read your research and papers, but you understand what's happening. People respect that and our viewers need to be aware of what's going to happen. By the way, the green area on the satellite? It's begun to shrink. I think the end might be in sight.'

I could have done without another visit to the set so soon after passing out on Friday but, once I'd shaken hands after the show was finished, I actually felt better than I had done in a long time. Madison elected to drive me home, where my parents and my lovely Emma were waiting. The winds had dropped by then.

I was glad Madison was doing the driving rather than Mom or Dad, as they were coping with a lot. Ryan was at the observatory, helping assess the damage and overseeing repairs. Also, he had that lecture tomorrow. I already felt more anxious about his well-being than I'd ever done with Josh. Maybe this was real love?

I laughed a little, realising that the pain from my ops was lessening. Maybe in a week or two, I could drive again and get back to work.

Once home, I was surprised to see that Maddy and my dad got on like a house on fire. She laughed at his lame jokes, genuinely finding them amusing. She had some home-made peach cobbler and a drink with the rest of us, mentioning that in England it was referred to as 'afternoon tea' traditionally at around this time of the day.

Our animated discussion included all sorts of things including anecdotes about her years across the pond in Britain. She made a point of including Emma in her conversation, explaining that 'no, I didn't meet the Queen' in answer to my little one's question.

Dad, in turn, wondered how she found their strange accents, confessing that whenever he and Mom watched British telly shows, they needed the subtitles on in order to understand.

All too soon, she decided it was time to get back to T-Town as the winds were picking up once more. Outside it was only thirty-eight degrees, uncharacteristically cold for this late in the spring. Emma and I waved as she set off up the road. Overhead, the skies were a dirty pale green.

The property damage had been wide-spread. There was talk of Federal Disaster Funding once the blue skies returned to Tulsa County.

★ ★ ★

The rest of Monday and most of Tuesday saw us experiencing three tornado alerts in the area. That was more than expected around us but par for the course with the Green Skies. I had expected most to be F1s but my climate model suggested at least one F5 in our county. Following our safety plan, we headed for the tornado shelter. Nothing happened, but it was better to take heed of the warnings.

By the time late afternoon came, the danger seemed to have gone. Maddy phoned to say that the circle of greenness on the sat photos was definitely shrinking.

Ryan phoned to say that the lecture had gone well. He asked if he and his grandfather, Red Bird, could come for dinner. Mom agreed, never one to be daunted by a few more mouths to feed.

I'd been concerned for the old man living by himself in this dreadful weather. Ryan had said he was in a tent, but surely that was a joke. The old-fashioned traditional ti-pi had made way for modern polyethylene equivalents in many cases. I wasn't totally ignorant of Cherokee customs. A ti-pi here was called an asi, was made of wattle and daub, and was more permanent as Cherokees were agricultural and didn't move much.

They both rolled up at about four-thirty in a cloud of dust. Each was in his own vehicle and I was amused to see that Red Bird was driving a very sporty Sixties Mustang. When I inquired about it, he smirked, maintaining that if it was fine for his venerated ancestors to ride mustangs, who was he to buck tradition?

Red Bird had seen a great deal of change in his lifetime. He was spry, though he admitted he was not as quick on his feet as he had once been.

Emma was fascinated by his unusual clothing and had to ask, especially about the feathers. Later Red Bird regaled us all with stories from the Cherokee Nation about giant inchworms and the Uhktena Serpent. 'We even have our own version of the Bible's Noah and the flood.'

This one had a dog speaking to forewarn a man of the rains. He built a raft and, stocked with provisions, saved his family.

Deluge stories appeared to be in so many cultures. For a moment, I wondered if these floods were linked to previous Green Skies. Forty days and nights of rain might be far too long though, considering the forces of nature that the Green Skies would have to disrupt.

'Your grandfather is so lovely and independent,' I said to Ryan as I kissed him prior to them both departing.

'Don't let him hear you say that. His health isn't great and I've been trying to get him to a care home. His ti-pi is a run-down old caravan in the bush not far from Pedro's house. No amenities, and the cold of the winter isn't helping his arthritis. Today is a good day for him. I worry a lot about him, Amber. He's the only family I have ... apart from you all.'

★ ★ ★

Over the next few days of sporadic winds and dry lightning storms, Ryan was busy most of the time. I missed him. On the positive side, the wild temperature fluctuations were settling down. Maddy reported on the television and to me about the imminent return of balmy spring days to Tulsa County. The circle of green visible on the satellite photos was almost a distant memory.

Finally, there was nothing left but a speck — barely visible from outer space — back where the strange pattern had begun two weeks earlier. Communication and transport links were restored and the skies were azure once more.

Ryan arrived in his Jeep one afternoon offering to take us for a late picnic. He was intending to visit Red Bird, and told Emma and me there was a great spot nearby where he often went for fishing and skinny-dipping. Not that either of those was on the agenda today, but we did take our bathing costumes along at his suggestion.

'There's a small waterfall, and we all need to relax after these past weeks. How are you recovering, Amber?'

Although I was tired of endless questions from everyone about my health, I understood that Ryan's were best-intentioned.

'Much better physically though there's a part of the old me that's missing in my mind. Self-confidence? I don't know. Something.' I buckled Emma in, next to the picnic basket and rug.

'Yeah, Amber. Obviously, I hadn't seen you since college but from what I've seen, you are more cautious. Dare I say it, I preferred the old you, ready to assert yourself more. I can't imagine you got as high up in the NWS by being such a pussycat. No offence.'

'No. You're right. Being with you and my parents hasn't helped. You are so protective... Not that that's a bad thing. Anyway. Shall we get going?'

'Yeah. But I swear, if I hear 'Are we there yet' from either of you two girls...'

★ ★ ★

The thirty-minute drive was pleasant. The flooded fields and occasional prairie were now a luxuriant, fresh green, the breeze sensuously caressing our hair through the open windows.

We sang songs like *Old McDonald*, with Ryan prompting Emma to choose the animal. She chose an elephant one time, which caused a problem until Ryan said 'Trumpet'. Singing '*With a trumpet, trumpet here*' and so on soon caused our verses to break down into laughter.

We had a whimsical break at the idyllic waterfall; eating, playing and swimming. The plan was to visit Red Bird's remote residence before returning home. It was after five. Ryan was telling Emma some terrible jokes but she found them funny. Amazingly, so did I. It was fun for us all.

Then I glanced out of the car window and stopped laughing. Ryan noticed.

'What's up, sweet-cheeks?'

I pointed to the horizon. 'That cloud formation over the hills. It's wrong.'

'How so? They're just clouds,' Ryan suggested.

I shook my head. 'Cumulo-nimbus … Thunderheads. But everywhere else we can see clouds they're cirrus; those wispy clouds like pure white strands of hair. I'm phoning Maddy.'

It was a relief that our cell phones were functioning properly once more. I'd felt lost without mine.

Maddy answered immediately.

'Amber. Just about to ring you. Trouble.'

'Out towards Shawnee? We're headed there now. Thunderheads. I'm guessing 40 or 50,000 feet. And they're expanding. The only consolation is, if they've been caused by the last remnant of the Green Skies, they won't move from where they are. It's very isolated out there.'

Ryan spoke. 'My grandfather's mobile

home is to the right. Well away from there, thank the stars. We should be there in ten minutes or so.'

I nodded before asking Maddy to keep us posted. This was the last hiccup of the meteorological disaster which had recently plagued us. It should blow itself out in hours ... if it stayed still.

The road turned into a gravel track as Ryan deftly turned right, heading up a hill. We were bounced around as if on a trampoline as the Jeep negotiated the numerous ruts and potholes. It was fortunate most of the puddles had dried up.

'How far up here?' I stuttered as my chest heaved up and down.

'Not far. A mile?' Ryan stuttered back. 'Pedro's ranch is not too distant. Where we went those first days, with the fulgurites, remember?'

We reached the crest of the hill and most of the trees we'd been driving through vanished as open grassland appeared. Emma and I both gasped. The views into the valley below were spectacular.

'I can see why Red Bird doesn't want to move from here to some pokey room in a rest home.'

'Actually, the rest home is for Cherokees only. It's spacious, with parkland. It would be perfect for him to be with his tribespeople. Sad to say, my grandfather is just an awkward, ornery coyote.'

★ ★ ★

Red Cloud's so-called ti-pi was hardly habitable; a 1970s mobile home that had seen far better days. It was well past the description 'a doer-upper'. More like a faller-downer.

I asked Ryan if its state of disrepair was down to the recent storms.

He told me, 'No. It's been like that for years. It's clean inside, though. Filled with memorabilia from the tribe,' Ryan half-apologised.

Then he showed concern. We'd had to park over a hundred yards away as Red Bird's Mustang was blocking the access. The motorhome was nestled in a copse of cedars near the top of the hill.

'That's strange. When he hears me arrive, he comes to greet me.' Slowly, then moving faster, he ran ahead, leaving me and Emma to clamber over the terrain after him. I heard a shout when he went inside. He returned to the makeshift door.

'Amber. He's injured.'

I held Emma's hand, walking as quickly as I could. My foot slipped on a mossy rock but I managed to regain my balance. By the time we'd arrived, I was panting from the exertion.

Inside it was obvious he'd fallen badly against the kitchenette cupboards. His forehead was bleeding. Then I saw the whiteness of bone tinged with crimson poking through his shirt. He'd broken his lower left arm, either the radius or ulna; I couldn't tell which.

He was dazed but coherent. Even so, he couldn't have managed to stand by himself. An overturned step ladder lay beside him on the floor.

'How long you been like this, Grandfather?' Ryan asked him as he knelt by the old man's side. He had some water in a glass that Red Bird sipped slowly. The heady scent of incense hung in the air.

'Since sun-up, my boy. Damn fool ladder.'

'Damn fool you. What on earth were you thinking?' Ryan replied calmly so as not to agitate him.

I heard Emma wanting to know what was wrong. It was best that she didn't come in. The blood might upset her.

'Ryan. Could you?' I said, nodding towards Emma.

'Can you help him, Amber?' He was quite worried. We needed to get him medical attention.

'My mom was a nurse. Setting a broken limb was one of the many things she taught me. All I need is something straight and strong, and sterile dressings.'

It was a clean, compound fracture. Luckily, Red Bird's first aid kit over the kitchen cupboard was well-stocked. The wide bandages could be wrapped around the padded splint I'd improvised.

'This is going to hurt a lot, Red Bird.'

'Amber. I've been shot by arrows. This'll be nothing,' he replied, gritting his teeth.

Carefully I moved the arm, reducing the break until the white bone was back inside his bloodied skin.

Wrapping it tightly was the next step. I was so intent on the task that I didn't notice the room getting darker.

'Amber?' Ryan sounded worried. 'Are we ready to get going?'

'A few more minutes, Ryan. Need to make sure he's stable.'

'Er … I don't think we have a few minutes. In fact, I think we need to all get inside … Now, Emma.' Without ceremony, he lifted my little girl in before stepping in too.

'Ryan? What are you doing?'

He frantically pulled the door closed, then the open skylight.

'What the … ' I yelled again as the first hailstone struck the skylight, cracking it clean across. Grabbing Emma to protect her, more loud bangs reverberated all over the mobile home as huge pimples appeared in the aluminium roof above.

Tentatively, I pulled aside the pristine net curtains in Red Bird's immaculate bijou home. Outside the ground was sparkling in the eerie green light. More shiny stones fell from the sky, dotting the landscape. Huge chunks of hail; some as large as my fist. No wonder Ryan had reacted as he did. We were under siege from the most violent ice-storm I'd ever witnessed.

I stared at clouds that were a dark, olive green, foreboding and intense. Moreover, they weren't moving. No — they were ... but very slowly despite the winds. Lightning lit the sky at times though the thunder was drowned out by the barrage of ice thump-thump-thumping on the fragile roof.

A window cracked at the other end of the van.

'I have to tell Maddy. Warn them all.

Get help,' I said loudly so as to be heard above the din. Emma and Red Bird were both cowering. In Red Bird's case, I suspected the pain from his injuries. Emma clung to my legs, whimpering.

'No signal.' The realisation that we were on our own without possibility of rescue consumed me for a moment. What could we expect to do against this heaven-sent apocalypse?

The skylight shattered, Perspex shards showering down around the ice stone now embedded in the carpeted floor. It had only just missed us.

'Quick. We need to get under shelter, Amber. The table.' Ryan grabbed Emma and pushed her beneath it, along with his grandfather. Turning to me, still stunned and immobile, he was struck by a smaller hailstone on the shoulder. He sank to his knees, holding it. His right arm hung loosely, blood soaking and spreading like ink on blotting paper over his checked, cotton shirt.

'Ryan!' I screamed, squatting next to him.

'Quick, Amber. Get yourselves under here,' Red Bird yelled above the screeching Banshee wind inside our sanctuary. By now the roof was a polka-dot of dents, joining up in places. Another window cracked as hail thudded against it.

'There's no room for everyone,' I said loudly, guiding Ryan, holding Emma, to crawl beneath the sturdy table. He was caught on his lower leg by yet another ice-ball, screaming in pain as it rolled away. Desperately, I squeezed him under, leaning dining chairs on the table to offer a semblance of further protection.

There clearly was no further room for me and the ceiling was now pockmarked with holes like a giant slab of Swiss cheese.

'Amber. Watch out,' Ryan shouted. I looked up as a huge sheet of the aluminium roof peeled back in the wind. Something was opening our sardine can of protection, exposing me to more danger. Everywhere I looked, there were puddles, lumps of ice and smashed furniture. There was nowhere else to hide. If this was the end for me, then at least my precious Emma was safe.

13

Green Skies at Night

Emma loved to hide. Where would she go? In the storage space beneath the bench seats? Maybe. There would be no room for me there. The bathroom? No. The ceiling would be as bad as this one. Then I saw it. The closet.

Sorry, Red Bird. I apologised silently, yanking his clothes from the rail. For some reason, there was a coil of rope on the floor. I tossed that out as well. There would be barely enough room, yet there was no choice. Unlike the flimsy light-wood doors of modern mobile homes, the entire coffin-like cupboard was made of solid wood. Moreover, there was a wooden ceiling, still intact.

I was aware that Ryan, at least, could see what I was doing. All of the time more ice rocks were crashing through the now fragmented roof. Any moment, one could hit me. The eerie glow of the clouds and sky was duller now that dusk was approaching.

It was so terrifying that I began to hyperventilate. Forcing myself to breathe slower was hard, especially as I pulled the door of the cupboard to. To close it completely was unthinkable, the Stygian blackness too much to bear. A half-inch of light was enough for me to see the others curled up beneath the table. At least I wasn't alone.

We all stayed like that for what seemed like days, each cramped and aching to stretch out yet unable to do so for fear of the hail crushing us.

What was worse was the winds tossing us around in the van, especially as one end of the van's supports had collapsed. At one stage the door hinge was hit and it started to come away. I grabbed it with both hands, realising my fingers might be vulnerable but there was no choice.

The home was being rocked back and forth, each time finishing on more of a slant. Twilight turned to night, the only illumination from the infrequent flashes of lightning or one of us opening our cell phones for a snatch of light or a peek at the time.

The thunderheads must have stalled again above us as it was after nine when I heard the din of hail striking all around begin to lessen. Tentatively, I pushed my door ajar.

'Is it over, Amber?' Ryan asked. His voice was raspy and weak.

'I doubt it. It's probably a break, like the eye of the hurricane. Listen. The winds have dropped. The eye is calm. If it had passed us by, the winds would be there. Is there a flashlight anywhere?'

'Two. Top drawer, right of the stove. Don't mess anything up, though. My home is my castle.'

It was Red Bird. Again, his voice was weak, hard to hear even though the hail had almost stopped. Despite the situation, I had to laugh at his dry humour.

'I figure you'll need to redecorate a bit, Red. Everyone stand up and let's get out of here. Just be careful of debris and the slippery floor.'

It was a struggle as the floor was at a precarious angle, so that we all had to hold on to move around. I passed one torch to Ryan, who took it with his good hand.

'You all right, kitten?' I said to Emma, holding her tightly. We'd survived this long. Now it was up to me to save us. Both Ryan and Red had their own injuries. They couldn't help.

'We have to leave here before the winds and hail return. I'll get the Jeep, Ryan. Obviously you can't. Get some painkillers and water. Food, if there is any. We all need our strength. I only hope it's drivable.'

He began to follow my directions as I took his keys and pushed what remained of the mobile-home door open. Tossing out the closet door, rope and anything else loose that was in my way, I surveyed the chaotic mess we were in.

I'd have to climb down as the door was about two feet higher now than the stone steps. I flashed the light towards where we'd left the Jeep. Melting ice glistened on the track leading there. The wreck of Red Bird's Mustang was half blown down a slope. The Jeep was relatively intact beneath a huge cedar that had protected it. A few branches lay broken, resting over the hood.

It was perilous walking down the now slippery track. It was only at that point could I see how precarious the caravan was, tilting as it was at the top of the hill.

We'd been lucky. Damned lucky. But the storm wasn't finished with us yet. The moon was starting to break through the clouds, which were an opalesque green circling above us. I'd been right about the literal eye of the storm.

More hail-laden clouds were visible and were destined to bring more destruction and terror to our neck of the wilderness.

Nearing the vehicle, I stumbled over some debris, falling forward. Instinctively, I put my hands forward to break my fall. It was a mistake. A shard of a broken tree cut into my left hand below the thumb.

Ryan must have heard my scream. His flashlight played over me.

'You OK, Amber?'

I stood up to survey the damage. There was a splinter of wood embedded there. It had to come out. No way could I drive with that.

'Just peachy,' I called out. 'It's nothing.'

I prayed it wasn't too deep. The anticoagulants should have gone now from my blood, allowing normal clotting. Even so.

It came out easily but quite painfully. Positioning the torch, I bound the wound with the dressing in my pocket, tying it with my teeth. The white changed to red, but the bleeding then seemed to stop. No time to waste. I had to hurry.

The Jeep engine coughed to life and I switched the lights on. There were holes in the thinner roof metal, but the hood cover over the motor was sound. I climbed in behind the wheel. It was all so much bigger than any car I'd driven.

Even the steering wheel was higher.

I figured that the windshield would shatter the minute it was hit by hailstones, leaving me and Ryan right in the firing line. It was a miracle it was still intact. As for driving through another storm without a window, my brain was convinced that we'd have no chance. Nevertheless, I had to try.

Revving the motor, I slipped the automatic gearbox into Drive and edged around the trunk of the Mustang, heading uphill gently over rocks to the mobile home and injured people with my Emma.

'Where are we going?' I asked Ryan as I alighted from the vehicle once I'd reached them. I'd left the engine running, the hand-brake on.

'Pedro has a storm shelter. I'll direct you.'

I burst into tears, holding him lightly. We kissed.

'I don't think I can do it, Ryan.'

'You have to, Amber. We can't. It's up to you.' He paused. Already the breeze had sprung up. The hail wouldn't be far behind. 'You've already done so much. You're strong. I love you.'

Disengaging himself from my clinging arms he hobbled painfully to the front of the Jeep, touching the windshield.

'It's strong. I had extra heavy-duty protective layers put on after it broke once from stone impact. We should be protected. We need something for the roof to protect the passengers, though. It's already punctured.'

'The closet doors. They saved me. And we'll use that rope to tie them to the inside.'

It was difficult given both men's arm injuries but we managed to tie the doors under the roof as they supported them, putting the rope through the windows and over the metal roof. Sitting inside, Red and Ryan had to duck their heads with the reduced roof space.

We all managed to buckle up as the renewed onslaught of hail commenced falling again.

'Ready?' I said, engaging Drive just as a violent gust of wind threw me against the driver's door. I groaned, touching my fingers to the injured hand. It was sticky.

Putting it back on the steering wheel, Ryan looked in horror at the black stain in the shadowy light inside the Jeep.

'Amber?'

I gritted my teeth.

'No choice. We're all dead, otherwise.'

Every bump now sent shards of pain shooting through my body. I wanted to close my eyes but I dared not. The trip down the winding road was hazardous – more so when parts of Red Bird's now shattered home blew across the track towards us.

After ages, we reached the main tarred road.

'Which way, Ryan?'

There was no answer. He was slumped in his seat by me, his phone loosely held in his hand.

'Take a right.' It was Red Bird. He shook Ryan, who moaned. At least he was alive. For the moment. 'Then second left, Amber. Then we're there. About two miles 'til the turn.'

One of the headlights was out, hit by hail. I switched on the phalanx of driving lights, though some of them had been damaged too. Broken branches and trees meant it was slow going.

'Hello. Pedro?' I heard Ryan's voice. Relief flooded through me. Concisely he managed to explain that we were injured and coming there. Then the cell phone slipped to the floor.

'Conserving strength. Been watching for a signal, Amber.' With my peripheral vision, I saw him grin. 'Looks like we'll make it, thanks to you.'

Pedro's ranch was in darkness but suddenly the outside lights came on. I saw a figure waving to us from under the shelter of the veranda. Another onslaught of the storm obliterated sight of him for a moment but then he was visible once more, much closer this time. The hail bouncing off the battered Jeep was noisy and the driving conditions horrendous but we'd soon all be safe.

I put my hand on Ryan's, squeezing it

lovingly. Whatever concerns I'd recently had about my own inner strength were gone — this time forever.

14

Going Back

Twelve weeks later, the four of us returned to the ruins of Red Bird's home. The summer had been the best I could remember but was almost over. As for the Green Skies, they had left us too, going to wherever such things go.

That night of terror had been the end of the damage wrought by our upside-down weather.

We stood to survey the spot where Red Bird's motorhome had once rested. We'd all talked about it, of course. I'd insisted. Red's arm was healing well, Ryan's shoulder too. Emma still had an occasional nightmare but, being at school, she had found support there to help her focus on new experiences and friends.

I'd transferred to Tulsa NWS. Already, I was loving it, working with Maddy and the others. 'Are you young 'uns certain you don't want to build here?' Red asked yet again. He'd moved into the retirement home and, despite his initial misgivings, was settling in well.

'Too far from work, Red. Besides, they're beginning building our new home next month. I'm certain that your fellow Cherokees will make full use of this land so it will still be in the family.'

He nodded. Those few traumatic weeks had taught all of us about love and priorities.

As for our new ranch, my parents had gifted us some land. Emma and I were looking forward to being there with Ryan.

'Penny for your thoughts, Amber,' Ryan said as we wandered around, hand in hand with Emma. The sound of birds gossiping and the scent of summer blooms stimulated my senses, reminding me of the good things in life that we'd almost lost.

'Just taking a moment to appreciate our blessings, my love. We've all had our share of stormy weather. We deserve more days like today with blue skies and fluffy clouds.'

We all ambled back to Ryan's new Jeep. He'd chosen a Cherokee this time and I was so pleased for him to be embracing this side of his heritage.

My cell phone buzzed. It was Madison.

'Hi ya, Amber. Just thought I'd inform you. There's been a new Green Skies report. France, of all places. The authorities have requested that you go over to advise them on how to proceed. What should I say?'

Ryan and Emma were watching a grasshopper jumping from rock to rock in the fields. I paused. Eventually, Maddy checked if I were still there.

'Sorry, babe. Just considering. The answer is no. I've had my fill of storms for awhiles. I can spare you, though. Ten days long enough? I'm sure you could do a report for your station, too.'

'Me? Go to France? You bet. Are you sure, Amber?'

'Yes … besides, you have all those collated records to take. You're the expert now.'

A few moments later, I wandered over to my new family.

'What do you think that cloud looks like?' I pointed. 'I figure a side-on giraffe.'

Everyone tipped their heads.

'Nonsense, Amber.' Red Bird disagreed. 'It's an eagle. See the wings?'

Ryan joined in. 'You're both right, kinda. Emma. What do you figure?'

Her response was so mature, I had to smile.

'I think we should lie on the grass and decide properly. There's no rush, is there?'

Emma lay down and studied the cloud intently, her little brow furrowed in concentration.

'It could be a birdie, or a giraffe. But to me, it's a fishy ... just like Nemo.'

We do hope that you have enjoyed reading this large print book.

Did you know that all of our titles are available for purchase?

We publish a wide range of high quality large print books including:
Romances, Mysteries, Classics
General Fiction
Non Fiction and Westerns

Special interest titles available in large print are:
The Little Oxford Dictionary
Music Book, Song Book
Hymn Book, Service Book

Also available from us courtesy of Oxford University Press:
Young Readers' Dictionary
(large print edition)
Young Readers' Thesaurus
(large print edition)

For further information or a free brochure, please contact us at:
Ulverscroft Large Print Books Ltd.,
The Green, Bradgate Road, Anstey,
Leicester, LE7 7FU, England.
Tel: (00 44) **0116 236 4325**
Fax: (00 44) **0116 234 0205**

TURPIN'S APPRENTICE

Sarah Swatridge

England, 1761. Charity Bell is the daughter of an inn keeper. Her two elder sisters are only interested in marrying well, whereas feisty Charity is determined to discover who the culprit is behind the most recent highwayman ambush. And by catching the highwayman, she aims to persuade Sir John to bring his family, and his wealth, to her village. It may also make the handsome Moses notice her!

THE NURSE AND THE CAPTAIN

Philippa Carey

It is 1918 and the Great War is ending. The evening before the last great battle, Ben hears that the flu epidemic has killed his entire family. Devastated, he is reckless in battle. Badly wounded, he is sent to an auxiliary hospital in England.

Laura's grandfather, the earl, has died, and she doesn't know what to do now. She volunteers at the local wartime hospital and is put in charge of a very sick officer …

REVENGE OF THE SPANISH PRINCESS

Linda Tyler

Cornwall, 1695. When her beloved father dies with the name Lovett on his lips, privateer captain Catherina Trelawny vows revenge on the mysterious pirate. Seeking him on the Mediterranean island of Azul, she is charmed by the personable Henry Darley. But Cate finds her plan goes awry when Darley and Lovett turn out to be the same man. Cate and Henry set sail across the high seas battling terrifying storms, deadly shipwreck, dissolute corsairs — and each other.

LOVE IN LAVENDER LANE

Jill Barry

Fiona exchanges her quiet suburban world for 1970s London when she inherits her great-aunt's marriage bureau near Marble Arch. But she has never been truly in love, so it's going to be a challenge arranging perfect pairings for her starry-eyed clients ... While Fiona's busy interviewing and arranging introductions, how will she ever find time to make her own dream come true? And could it be that she and her most difficult client to match are actually meant for one another?

THE LOVE TREE

Patricia Keyson

When Lily arrives at The Limes to work as a maid for two sisters, Eta and Mabel, little does she know she will instantly fall in love with their handsome lodger, Samuel. When Cecil Potts visits the sisters' beer house and shop, a tale of murder, death and deceit unravels. Will Lily and Samuel ever step out from Cecil's dark shadow to find happiness under the love tree?